Happy Families

HAPPY FAMILIES

EDITED BY

BARBARA WILLARD

ILLUSTRATED BY

KRYSTYNA TURSKA

MACMILLAN PUBLISHING CO., INC.
New York

First published in Great Britain 1974 by Hamish Hamilton Children's Books Ltd.

Copyright © 1974 in this collection Barbara Willard

Illustrations Copyright © 1974 Krystyna Turska

Macmillan Publishing Co., Inc., 866 Third Avenue, New York, N.Y. 10022

The acknowledgments on pages 255–256 constitute an extension of this copyright page.

Printed in Great Britain
First American Edition

Library of Congress Cataloging in Publication Data

Willard, Barbara, comp.   Happy families.
    1. Children's literature (Collections) [1. Short stories. 2. Family life—Fiction]
I. Turska, Krystyna, 1933– illus. II. Title.   PZ5.W638Hap3   820'.8'0355 [Fic]
73-22433   ISBN 0-02-793010-6

Contents

5

6 CONTENTS

Introduction

It is commonly expected of all families that they should be happy ones. Differences—if any—must be confined to the privacy of home, while to the outside world there is presented a pleasant row of faces, all smiling furiously . . . So our great-grandparents saw it, and their great-grandparents before them. Out of this idea arises a familiar catchphrase that may be applied to almost any group of people: *They are just one big happy family*. It is indeed a fact that happiness and families should go hand in hand, for nowhere but at home can one particular kind of easy comfortable manners be enjoyed. However, the time is past when it need be pretended that all little birds in the nest agree, or to deny that a good roaring, snapping family row may offer satisfactions and amusements of its own.

Probably the most important single thing to be said about families is that they will hang together in the face of an enemy and defend one another despite the most formidable opposition. They will do this, not a doubt of it, even when they are at odds among themselves. This is called *family feeling*. Since our particular society has been built up over centuries on the family in matters of property and so on, family ties will always be upheld in law.

Families have varied enormously at different periods in time. There used to be huge numbers of babies born, but not so many of them survived when medicine was still rather primitive. You can see family tombs in parish churches all over the country showing all the children born to a family, some carrying little skulls to show that they died young. Still, they are not forgotten,

7

though their parents can have had little time to mourn them before the cradle filled up with the next one. In a later age, one of the most touching family remarks comes from the child in Wordsworth's poem who says "We are seven", but adds that "two in the church-yard lie".

In Victorian times medicine was improving so more children survived, and large families were the rule. Members of small families are inclined to think of big ones as automatically happy, imagining with envy their endless games and adventures. Yet often in such a family the youngest and the eldest can be strangers, for the eldest are out into the world and careering heaven knows where by the time the youngest have begun to look around.

This book is concerned with families real and invented, in prose and verse. They are not always in neat sets of Mr and Mrs, Master and Miss, as in the game of *Happy Families* which can so usefully help over wet days or boring stretches of after-measles. Families divide themselves in many ways. They may consist at any one time entirely of aunts and nephews or uncles and nieces, or may suddenly expand to embrace cousins in dozens and grandparents in pairs, as at Christmas gatherings. They may just as well be reduced to two sisters, or father and son, or four brothers and a grandmother, or brother and sister, or mother and five daughters, or eight cousins—the computations are endless. Nor should the only child forget that it bears the responsibility of being a family of one.

It would be impossible to include in a book light enough to handle all the—mostly—happy families that come to mind. Most of those mentioned here can be read of at greater length inside their own covers; which could be a useful contribution to family living—for most reading families, I truly believe, are happy ones.

Barbara Willard

Happy Families

A Prayer for a Happy Family

URSULA MORAY WILLIAMS

God bless Mum and Dad and Baby
God bless me and sister Sue.
God bless Auntie Bloss, and maybe
Bless my Uncle Ernest too.
God bless Granma, God bless Grandy,
God bless cousins Dick and Dot.
God bless Marge and little Mandy,
Though you needn't bless a lot.
Bless my home and bless my teacher,
Stop her telling tales to Mum.
Bless Aunt Rose if you can reach her
Safe at rest in Kingdom Come.
Bless my family and guard them
Keep them safe and free from sin.
Now that's finished we'll discard them,
This is where my prayers begin:

PLEASE GOD DO LET AUNTIE BLOSS ASK GRANMA TO TELL
MUM TO MAKE DAD SAY I REALLY CAN KEEP A RABBIT.

The History of the Fairchild Family

MRS. SHERWOOD

Appearing in three parts from 1818–1847, this may well be one of the earliest family stories for children that was actually published. This is how the story starts:

Mr and Mrs Fairchild lived very far from any town; their house stood in the midst of a garden, which in the summer time was full of fruit and sweet flowers. Mr Fairchild kept only two servants, Betty and John: Betty's business was to clean the house, cook the dinner, and milk the cow; and John waited at table, worked in the garden, fed the pig, and took care of the meadow in which the cow grazed.

Mr and Mrs Fairchild had three children: Lucy, who was about nine years old when these stories began; Emily, who was next in age; and Henry, who was between six and seven. These little children did not go to school: Mrs Fairchild taught Lucy and Emily, and Mr Fairchild taught little Henry. Lucy and Emily learned to read, and to do various kinds of needlework. Lucy had begun to write, and took great pains with her writing; their mamma also taught them to sing psalms and hymns, and they could sing several very sweetly. Little Henry, too, had a great notion of singing.

Besides working and reading, the little girls could do many useful things; they made their beds, rubbed the chairs and tables in their rooms, fed the fowls; and when John was busy, they laid the cloth for dinner, and were ready to fetch anything which their papa or mamma might want.

Mr Fairchild taught Henry everything that was proper for little boys in his station to know; and when he had finished his lessons in the morning, his papa used to take him very often to work in the garden; for Mr Fairchild had great pleasure in helping John to keep the garden clean. Henry had a little basket, and he used to carry the weeds and rubbish in his basket out of the garden, and do many such other little things as his papa set him to do.

I must not forget to say that Mr Fairchild had a school for poor boys in the next village, and Mrs Fairchild one for girls.

I do not mean that they taught the children entirely themselves, but they paid a master and mistress to teach them; and they used to take a walk two or three times a week to see the children, and to give rewards to those who had behaved well. When Lucy and Emily and Henry were obedient, their papa and mamma were so kind as to let them go with them to see the schools; and then they always contrived to have some little thing ready to carry with them, as presents to the good children . . .

If you want more, there is plenty of it. The Fairchilds are smug, pious, self-righteous prigs. With such parents, how can the poor little things be otherwise? Mr Fairchild is often cruel, while Mrs Fairchild quite clearly looks upon herself as a sort of angel-on-earth. Poor Lucy, Emily and Henry can hardly hope to grow up much different—though there is just a chance that Henry might turn out to be a bad lot, and that would not be his fault. However, if in spite of all this you read the book, you will find a number of lively and rebellious lesser characters, all of whom are intended by their author, Mrs Sherwood, to point the excellence of the Fairchilds. To our less reverent eyes they seem to do precisely the opposite. The Fairchilds so obviously look upon themselves as a Happy Family, that to leave them out of this book would seem, as Mr Fairchild himself would most certainly say, a sad dereliction of duty.

From *The History of the Fairchild Family* (1818–1847)

A Happy Family

JULIANA HORATIA EWING

"If solid happiness we prize,
　Within our breast this jewel lies.

·　　·　　·　　·　　·　　·

From our own selves our joys must flow,
　And peace begins at home."

Cotton

The family—our family, not the Happy Family—consisted of
me and my brothers and sisters. I have a father and mother,
of course.

I am the eldest, as I remind my brothers; and of the more
worthy gender, which my sisters sometimes forget. Though
we live in the village, my father is a gentleman, as I shall be
when I am grown up. I have told the village boys so more
than once. One feels mean in boasting that one is better born
than they are; but if I did not tell them, I am not sure that
they would always know.

Our house is old, and we have a ghost—the ghost of my
great-great-great-great-great-aunt.

She "crossed her father's will," nurse says, and he threatened to flog her with his dog-whip, and she ran away, and

15

was never heard of more. He would not let the pond be dragged, but he never went near it again; and the villagers do not like to go near it now. They say you may meet her there, after sunset, flying along the path among the trees, with her hair half down, and a knot of ribbon fluttering from it, and parted lips, and terror in her eyes.

The men of our family (my father's family, my mother is Irish) have always had strong wills. I have a strong will myself.

People say I am like the picture of my great-grandfather (the great-great-great-nephew of the ghost). He must have been a wonderful old gentleman by all accounts. Sometimes nurse says to us, "Have your own way, and you'll live the longer," and it always makes me think of great-grandfather,

who had so much of his own way, and lived to be nearly a hundred.

I remember my father telling us how his sisters had to visit their old granny for months at a time, and how he shut the shutters at three o'clock on summer afternoons, and made them play dummy whist by candle light.

"Didn't you and your brothers go?" asked Uncle Patrick, across the dinner-table. My father laughed.

"Not we! My mother got us there once—but never again."

"And did your sisters like it?"

"Like it? They used to cry their hearts out. I really believe it killed poor Jane. She was consumptive and chilly, but always craving for fresh air; and granny never would have open windows, for fear of draughts on his bald head; and yet the girls had no fires in their room, because young people shouldn't be pampered."

"And ye never-r offer-r-ed—neither of ye—to go in the stead of them?"

When Uncle Patrick rolls his R's in a discussion, my mother becomes nervous.

"One can't expect boys to consider things," she said. "Boys will be boys, you know."

"And what would you have 'em be?" said my father. Uncle Patrick turned to my mother.

"Too true, Geraldine. Ye don't expect it. Worse luck! I assure ye, I'd be aghast at the brutes we men can be, if I wasn't more amazed that we're as good as we are, when the best and gentlest of your sex—the moulders of our childhood, the desire of our manhood—demand so little for all that you alone can give. There were conceivable uses in women preferring the biggest brutes of barbarous times, but it's not so now; and boys will be civilised boys, and men will be civilised men, sweet sister, when you *do* expect it, and when your grace and favours are the rewards of nobleness, and not the easy prize of selfishness and savagery."

My father spoke fairly.

"There's some truth in what you say, Pat."

"And small grace in my saying it. Forgive me, John."

That's the way Uncle Patrick flares up and cools down, like a straw bonfire. But my father makes allowances for him; first, because he is an Irishman, and, secondly, because he's a cripple.

. . . .

I love my mother dearly, and I can do anything I like with her. I always could. When I was a baby, I would not go to sleep unless she walked about with me, so (though walking was bad for her) I got my own way, and had it afterwards.

With one exception. She would never tell me about my godfather. I asked once, and she was so distressed that I was glad to promise never to speak of him again. But I only thought of him the more, though all I knew about him was his portrait—such a fine fellow—and that he had the same swaggering, ridiculous name as mine.

How my father allowed me to be christened Bayard I cannot imagine. But I was rather proud of it at one time—in the days when I wore long curls, and was so accustomed to hearing myself called "a perfect picture", and to having my little sayings quoted by my mother and her friends, that it made me miserable if grown-up people took the liberty of attending to anything but me. I remember wriggling myself off my mother's knee when I wanted change, and how she gave me her watch to keep me quiet, and stroked my curls, and called me her fair-haired knight, and her little Bayard; though, remembering also, how lingeringly I used just not to do her bidding, ate the sugar when she wasn't looking, tried to bawl myself into fits, kicked the nurse-girl's shins, and dared not go upstairs by myself after dark—I must confess that a young chimpanzee would have as good claims as I had to represent that model of self-conquest and true chivalry, "the Knight without fear and without reproach."

However, the vanity of it did not last long. I wonder if that grand-faced godfather of mine suffered as I suffered when he went to school and said his name was Bayard? I owe a day in harvest to the young wag who turned it into Backyard. I gave in my name as Backyard to every subsequent inquirer, and Backyard I modestly remained.

·　·　·　·　·　·　·　·　·

CHAPTER II

"The lady with the gay macaw."
Longfellow

My sisters are much like other fellows' sisters, excepting Lettice. That child is like no one but herself.

I used to tease the other girls for fun, but I teased Lettice on principle—to knock the nonsense out of her. She was only eight, and very small, but, from the top row of her tight little curls to the rosettes on her best shoes, she seemed to me a mass of affectation.

Strangers always liked Lettice. I believe she was born with a company voice in her mouth; and she would flit like a butterfly from one grown-up person to another, chit-chattering, whilst some of us stood pounding our knuckles in our pockets, and tying our legs into knots, as we wished the drawing-room carpet would open and let us through into the cellar to play at catacombs.

That was how Cocky came. Lettice's airs and graces bewitched the old lady who called in the yellow chariot, and was so like a cockatoo herself—a cockatoo in a citron velvet bonnet, with a bird of Paradise feather. When that old lady put up her eye-glass, she would have frightened a yard-dog; but Lettice stood on tip-toes, and stroked the feather, saying, "What a love-e-ly bird!" And next day came Cocky—perch and all complete—*for the little girl who loves birds*. Lettice was proud of Cocky, but Edward really loved him, and took trouble with him.

Edward is a good boy. My mother called him after the Black Prince.

He and I disgraced ourselves in the eyes of the Cockatoo lady, and it cost the family thirty thousand pounds, which we can ill afford to lose. It was unlucky that she came to luncheon the very day that Edward and I had settled to dress up as Early Britons, in blue woad, and dine off earthnuts in the shrubbery. As we slipped out at the side door, the yellow chariot drove up to the front. We had doormats on, as well as powder-blue, but the old lady was terribly shocked, and drove straight away, and did not return. Nurse says she is my father's godmother, and has thirty thousand pounds, which she would have bequeathed to us if we had not offended her. I take the blame entirely, because I always made the others play as I pleased.

We used to play at all kinds of things—concerts, circuses, theatricals, and sometimes conjuring. Uncle Patrick had not been to see us for a long time, when one day we heard that he was coming, and I made up my mind at once that I would have a perfectly new entertainment for him.

We like having entertainments for Uncle Patrick, because he is such a very good audience. He laughs, and cries, and claps, and thumps with his crutch, and if things go badly, he amuses the rest.

Ever since I can remember anything, I remember an old print, called "The Happy Family" over our nursery fireplace, and how I used to wonder at that immovable cat, with sparrows on her back, sitting between an owl and a magpie. And it was when I saw Edward sitting with Benjamin the cat, and two sparrows he had brought up by hand, struggling and laughing because Cocky would push itself, crest first, under his waistcoat, and come out at the top to kiss him—that an idea struck me; and I resolved to have a

Happy Family for Uncle Patrick, and to act Showman myself.

Edward can do anything with beasts. He was absolutely
necessary as confederate, but it was possible Lettice might
want to show off with Cocky, and I did not want a girl on
the stage, so I said very little to her. But I told Edward to
have in the yard-dog, and practise him in being happy with
the rest of the family pets. Fred, the farm-boy, promised to
look out for an owl. Benjamin, the cat, could have got mice
enough; but he would have eaten them before Edward had
had time to teach him better, so I set a trap. I knew a village-
boy with a magpie, ready tamed.

Bernard, the yard-dog, is a lumbering old fellow, with no
tricks. We have tried. We took him out once, into a snow-
drift, with a lantern round his neck, but he rescued nothing,
and lost the lantern—and then he lost himself, for it was
dark.

But he is very handsome and good, and I knew, if I put
him in the middle, he would let anything sit upon him. He
would not feel it, or mind if he did. He takes no notice of
Cocky.

Benjamin never quarrels with Cocky, but he dare not forget that Cocky is there. And Cocky sometimes looks at
Benjamin's yellow eyes as if it were thinking how very easily
they would come out. But they are quite sufficiently happy
together for a Happy Family.

The mice gave more trouble than all the rest, so I settled
that Lettice should wind up the mechanical mouse, and run
that on as the curtain rose.

CHAPTER III

Do you wish to avoid vexations? Then never have a Happy Family! Mine were countless.

Fred could not get me an owl. Lettice *did* want to show off with Cocky. I had my own way, but she looked sulky and spiteful. I got Tom Smith's magpie; but I had to have him, too. However, my costume as Showman was gorgeous, and Edward kept our Happy Family well together. We arranged that Tom should put Mag on at the left wing, and then run round behind, and call Mag softly from the right. Then she would hop across the stage to him, and show off well. Lettice was to let mother know when the spectators might take their places, and to tell the gardener when to raise the curtain.

I really think one magpie must be "a sign of sorrow," as nurse says; but what made Bernard take it into his beautiful foolish head to give trouble I cannot imagine. He wouldn't lie down, and when he did, it was with a *grump* of protest that seemed to forbode failure. However, he let Cocky scold him and pull his hair, which was a safety-valve for Cocky. Benjamin dozed with dignity. He knew Cocky wasn't watching for his yellow eyes.

I don't think Lettice meant mischief when she summoned the spectators, for time was up. But her warning the curtain to rise when it did was simple malice and revenge.

I never can forget the catastrophe, but I do not clearly remember how Tom Smith and I *began* to quarrel. He was excessively impudent, and seemed to think we couldn't have had a Happy Family without him and his chattering senseless magpie.

When I told him to remember he was speaking to a gentleman, he grinned at me.

"A gentleman? Nay, my sakes! Ye're not civil enough by half. More like a new policeman, if ye weren't such a Guy Fawkes in that finery."

"Be off," said I, "and take your bird with you."

"What if I won't go?"

"I'll make you!"

"Ye darsen't touch me."

"Daren't I?"

"Ye darsen't."

"I dare."

"Try."

"*Are* you going?"

"Noa."

I only pushed him. He struck first. He's bigger than me, but he's a bigger coward, and I'd got him down in the middle of the stage, and had given him something to bawl about, before I became conscious that the curtain was up. I only realised it then, because civil, stupid Fred arrived at the left wing, panting and gasping—

"Measter Bayard! Here's a young wood-owl for ye."

As he spoke, it escaped him, fluff and feathers flying in the effort, and squawking, plunging, and fluttering, made wildly for the darkest corner of the stage, just as Lettice ran on the mechanical mouse in front.

Bernard rose, and shook off everything, and Cocky went into screaming hysterics; above which I now heard the thud of Uncle Patrick's crutch, and the peals upon peals of laughter with which our audience greeted my long-planned spectacle of a Happy Family!

.　　.　　.　　.　　.　　.　　.　　.　　.

Our Irish uncle is not always nice. He teases and mocks, and has an uncertain temper. But one goes to him in trouble. I went next morning to pour out my woes, and defend myself, and complain of the others.

I spoke seriously about Lettice. It is not pleasant for a fellow to have a sister who grows up peculiar, as I believe Lettice will. Only the Sunday before, I told her she would be just the sort of woman men hate, and she said she didn't care; and I said she ought to, for women were made for men, and the Bible says so; and she said grandmamma said that every soul was made for GOD and its own final good. She was in a high-falutin mood, and said she wished she had been christened Joan instead of Lettice, and that I would be a true Bayard; and that we could ride about the world together, dressed in armour, and fighting for the right. And she would say all through the list of her favourite heroines, and asked me if I minded *their* being peculiar, and I said of course not, why should you mind what women do who don't belong to you? So she said she could not see that; and I said that was because girls can't see reason; and so we quarrelled, and I gave her a regular lecture, which I repeated to Uncle Patrick.

He listened quite quietly till my mother came in, and got fidgety, and told me not to argue with my uncle. Then he said—

"Ah! let the boy talk, Geraldine, and let me hear what he has to say for himself. There's a sublime audacity about his notions, I tell ye. Upon me conscience, I believe he thinks his grandmother was created for his particular convenience."

That's how he mocks, and I suppose he meant my Irish grandmother. He thinks there's nobody like her in the wide world, and my father says she is the handsomest and wittiest old lady in the British Isles. But I did not mind. I said,

"Well, Uncle Patrick, you're a man, and I believe you agree with me, though you mock me."

"Agree with ye?" He started up, and pegged about the room. "Faith! if the life we live is like the globe we inhabit— if it revolves on its own axis, *and you're that axis*—there's not a flaw in your philosophy; but IF—— Now perish my impetuosity! I've frightened your dear mother away. May I ask, by the bye, if she has the good fortune to please ye, since the Maker of all souls made her, for all eternity, with the particular object of mothering you in this brief patch of time?"

He had stopped under the portrait—my godfather's portrait. All his Irish rhodomontade went straight out of my head, and I ran to him.

"Uncle, you know I adore her! But there's one thing she won't do, and, oh, I wish you would! It's years since she told me never to ask, and I've been on honour, and I've never even asked nurse; but I don't think it's wrong to ask you. Who is that man behind you, who looks such a wonderfully fine fellow? My Godfather Bayard."

I had experienced a shock the night before, but nothing to the shock of seeing Uncle Patrick's face then, and hearing him sob out his words, instead of their flowing like a stream.

"Is it possible? Ye don't know? She can't speak of him yet? Poor Geraldine!"

He controlled himself, and turned to the picture, leaning on his crutch. I stood by him and gazed too, and I do not think, to save my life, I could have helped asking—

"Who is he?"

"Your uncle. Our only brother. Oh, Bayard, Bayard!"

"Is he dead?"

He nodded, speechless; but somehow I could not forbear.
"What did he die of?"

"Of unselfishness. He died—for others."

"Then he *was* a hero? That's what he looks like. I am glad
he is my godfather. Dear Uncle Pat, do tell me all about it."

"Not now—hereafter. Nephew, any man—with the heart
of a man and not of a mouse—is more likely than not to
behave well at a pinch; but no man who is habitually selfish
can be *sure* that he will, when the choice comes sharp between his own life and the lives of others. The impulse of a
supreme moment only focuses the habits and customs of a
man's soul. The supreme moment may never come, but
habits and customs mould us from the cradle to the grave.
His were early disciplined by our dear mother, and he
bettered her teaching. Strong for the weak, wise for the
foolish—tender for the hard—gracious for the surly—good
for the evil. Oh, my brother, without fear and without
reproach! Speak across the grave, and tell your sister's
son that vice and cowardice become alike impossible to a
man who has never—cradled in selfishness, and made
callous by custom—learned to pamper himself at the expense
of others!"

I waited a little before I asked—

"Were you with him when he died?"

"I was."

"Poor Uncle Patrick! What *did* you do?"

He pegged away to the sofa, and threw himself on it.

"Played the fool. Broke an arm and a thigh, and damaged
my spine, and—*lived*. Here rest the mortal remains."

And for the next ten minutes, he mocked himself, as he only can.

.   .   .   .

One does not like to be outdone by an uncle, even by such an uncle; but it is not very easy to learn to live like God-father Bayard.

Sometimes I wish my grandmother had not brought up her sons to such a very high pitch, and sometimes I wish my mother had let that unlucky name become extinct in the family, or that I might adopt my nickname. One could live up to *Backyard* easily enough. It seems to suit being grumpy and tyrannical, and seeing no further than one's own nose, so well.

But I do try to learn unselfishness; though I sometimes think it would be quite as easy for the owl to learn to respect the independence of a mouse, or a cat to be forbearing with a sparrow!

I certainly get on better with the others than I used to do; and I have some hopes that even my father's godmother is not finally estranged through my fault.

Uncle Patrick went to call on her whilst he was with us. She is very fond of "that amusing Irishman with the crutch," as she calls him; and my father says he'll swear Uncle Patrick entertained her mightily with my unlucky entertainment, and that she was as pleased as Punch that her cockatoo was in the thick of it.

I am afraid it is too true; and the idea made me so hot, that if I had known she was really coming to call on us again, I should certainly have kept out of the way. But when Uncle Patrick said, "If the yellow chariot rolls this way again, Bayard, ye need not be pursuing these archaeological revivals of yours in a too early English costume," I thought it was only his chaff. But she did come.

I was pegging out the new gardens for the little ones. We were all there, and when she turned her eye over us (just like a cockatoo), and said, in a company voice—

"What a happy little family!"

I could hardly keep my countenance, and I heard Edward choking in Benjamin's fur, where he had hidden his face.

But Lettice never moved a muscle. She clasped her hands, and put her head to one side, and said—in *her* company voice—"But you know brother Bayard *is* so good to us now, and *that* is why we are such A HAPPY FAMILY."

From *Melchior's Dream and Other Tales* (1886)

The Poor Cottages

FRANCES HODGSON BURNETT

Frances Hodgson Burnett, who was born in 1894 and died in 1924, is best known to us now by The Secret Garden. *But for years and years,* Little Lord Fauntleroy *was by far her most popular book. For some time it has been hard to stomach a lad with long golden curls who calls his mother Dearest, and so the book has been neglected. Take it out again—it is a marvellous story, and Cedric is no longer the only boy in the world without short hair. And if there are some sloppy moments they are perfectly balanced by the asperities of the tetchy old Lord Dorincourt, Cedric's grandfather. Having quarrelled with his son and heir for marrying an American, the old man is very reluctant indeed to be beguiled by Cedric—by the time this extract is reached, however, the process is well on its way . . .*

The fact was, his lordship the Earl of Dorincourt thought in those days of many things of which he had never thought before, and all his thoughts were in one way or another connected with his grandson. His pride was the strongest part of his nature, and the boy gratified it at every point. Through this pride he began to find a new interest in life. He began to take pleasure in showing his heir to the world. The world had known of his disappointment in his sons; so there was an agreeable touch of triumph in exhibiting this new Lord

Fauntleroy, who could disappoint no one. He wished the child to appreciate his own power and to understand the splendour of his position; he wished that others should realise it, too. He made plans for his future. Sometimes in secret he actually found himself wishing that his own past life had been a better one, and that there had been less in it that this pure, childish heart would shrink from if it knew the truth. It was not agreeable to think how the beautiful innocent face would look if its owner should be made to understand that his grandfather had been called for many a year "the wicked Earl of Dorincourt". The thought even made him feel a trifle nervous. He did not wish the boy to find it out. Sometimes in this new interest he forgot his gout, and after a while his doctor was surprised to find his noble patient's health growing better than he had expected it would ever be again. Perhaps the Earl grew better because the time did not pass so slowly for him, and he had something to think of besides his pains and infirmities.

One fine morning, people were amazed to see little Lord Fauntleroy riding his pony with another companion than Wilkins. This new companion rode a tall, powerful grey horse, and was no other than the Earl himself. It was, in fact, Fauntleroy who had suggested this plan. As he had been on the point of mounting his pony he had said rather wistfully to his grandfather:

"I wish you were going with me. When I go away I feel lonely because you are left all by yourself in such a big castle. I wish you could ride too."

And the greatest excitement had been aroused in the stables a few minutes later by the arrival of an order that Selim was to be saddled for the Earl. After that, Selim was saddled almost every day; and the people became accustomed to the sight of the tall grey horse carrying the tall grey old man with his handsome, fierce, eagle face, by the side of the brown pony which bore little Lord Fauntleroy. And in their rides together through the green lanes and the pretty country roads, the two riders became more intimate than ever. And gradually the old man heard a great deal about "Dearest" and her life. As Fauntleroy trotted by the big horse he chatted gaily. It was he who talked the most. The Earl often was silent, listening and watching the joyous, glowing face. Sometimes he would tell his young companion to set the pony off at a gallop, and when the little fellow dashed off, sitting so straight and fearless, he would watch the boy with a gleam of pride and pleasure in his eyes; and Fauntleroy when, after such a dash, he came back waving his cap with a laughing shout, always felt that he and his grandfather were very good friends indeed.

One thing that the Earl discovered was that his son's wife did not lead an idle life. It was not long before he learned that the poor people knew her very well indeed. When there was sickness or sorrow or poverty in any house, the little brougham often stood before the door.

"Do you know," said Fauntleroy once, "they all say 'God bless you!' when they see her, and the children are glad. There are some who go to her house to be taught to sew. She says she feels so rich now that she wants to help the poor ones."

It had not displeased the Earl to find that the mother of his heir had a beautiful young face and looked as much like a lady as if she had been a duchess, and in one way it did not displease him to know that she was popular and beloved by the poor. And yet he was often conscious of a hard, jealous pang when he saw how she filled her child's heart and how the boy clung to her as his best beloved. The old man would have desired to stand first himself and have no rival.

That same morning he drew up his horse on an elevated point of the moor over which they rode, and made a gesture with his whip, over the broad, beautiful landscape spread before them.

"Do you know that all that land belongs to me?" he said to Fauntleroy.

"Does it?" answered Fauntleroy. "How much it is to belong to one person, and how beautiful!"

"Do you know that some day it will all belong to you— that and a great deal more?"

"To me?" exclaimed Fauntleroy, in a rather awe-stricken voice. "When?"

"When I am dead," his grandfather answered.

"Then I don't want it," said Fauntleroy. "I want you to live always."

"That's kind," answered the Earl in his dry way; "nevertheless, some day it will all be yours—some day you will be the Earl of Dorincourt."

Little Lord Fauntleroy sat very still in his saddle for a few moments. He looked over the broad moors, the green farms, the beautiful copses, the cottages in the lanes, the pretty village, and over the trees to where the turrets of the great castle rose, grey and stately. Then he gave a queer little sigh.

"What are you thinking of?" asked the Earl.

"I am thinking," replied Fauntleroy, "what a little boy I am! and of what Dearest said to me."

"What was it?" enquired the Earl.

"She said that perhaps it was not so easy to be very rich; that if anyone had so many things always, one might sometimes forget that every one else was not so fortunate, and that one who is rich should always be careful and try to remember. I was talking to her about how good you were, and she said that was such a good thing, because an earl had

so much power, and if he cared only about his own pleasure and never thought about the people who lived on his lands, they might have trouble that he could help—and there were so many people, and it would be such a hard thing. And I was just looking at all those houses, and thinking how I should have to find out about the people when I was an earl. How did you find out about them?"

As his lordship's knowledge of his tenantry consisted in finding out which of them paid their rent promptly, and in turning out those who did not, this was rather a hard question. "Newick finds out for me," he said, and he pulled his great grey moustache, and looked at his small questioner rather uneasily. "We will go home now," he added; "and when you are an Earl, see to it that you are a better one than I have been."

He was very silent as they rode home. He felt it to be almost incredible that he, who had never really loved anyone in his life, should find himself growing so fond of this little fellow—as without doubt he was. At first he had only been pleased and proud of Cedric's beauty and bravery, but there was something more than pride in his feeling now. He laughed a grim, dry laugh all to himself sometimes, when he thought how he liked to have the boy near him, how he liked to hear his voice, and how in secret he really wished to be liked and thought well of by his small grandson.

"I'm an old fellow in my dotage, and I have nothing else to think of," he would say to himself; and yet he knew it was not that altogether. And if he had allowed himself to admit the truth, he would perhaps have found himself obliged to own that the very things which attracted him, in spite of himself, were the qualities he had never possessed—the frank, true, kindly nature, the affectionate trustfulness which could never think evil.

It was only about a week after that ride when, after a visit to his mother, Fauntleroy came into the library with a troubled, thoughtful face. He sat down in that high-backed chair in which he had sat on the evening of his arrival, and for a while he looked at the embers on the hearth. The Earl watched him in silence, wondering what was coming. It was evident that Cedric had something on his mind. At last he looked up. "Does Newick know all about the people?" he asked.

"It is his business to know about them," said his lordship. "Been neglecting it—has he?"

Contradictory as it may seem, there was nothing which entertained and edified him more than the little fellow's interest in his tenantry. He had never taken any interest in them himself, but it pleased him well enough that, with all his childish habits of thought and in the midst of all his childish amusements and high spirits, there should be such a quaint seriousness working in the curly head.

"There is a place," said Fauntleroy, looking up at him with wide-open, horror-stricken eyes—"Dearest has seen it; it is at the other end of the village. The houses are close together and almost falling down; you can scarcely breathe; and the people are so poor and everything is dreadful! Often they have fever, and the children die; and it makes them wicked to live like that, and be so poor and miserable! It is worse than Michael and Bridget! The rain comes in at the roof! Dearest went to see a poor woman who lived there. She would not let me come near her until she had changed all her things. The tears ran down her cheeks when she told me about it!"

The tears had come into his own eyes, but he smiled through them.

"I told her you didn't know, and I would tell you," he

said. He jumped down and came and leaned against the Earl's chair. "You can make it all right," he said, "just as you made it all right for Higgins. You always make it all right for everybody. I told her you would, and that Newick must have forgotten to tell you."

The Earl looked down at the hand on his knee. Newick had not forgotten to tell him; in fact, Newick had spoken to him more than once of the desperate condition of the end of the village known as Earl's Court. He knew all about the tumble-down, miserable cottages, and the bad drainage, and the damp walls and broken windows and leaking roofs, and all about the poverty, the fever and the misery. Mr Mordaunt had painted it all to him in the strongest words he could use, and his lordship had used violent language in response; and, when his gout had been at the worst, he had said that the sooner the people of Earl's Court died and were buried by the parish the better it would be—and there was an end of the matter. And yet, as he looked at the small hand on his knee, and from the small hand to the honest, earnest, frank-eyed face, he was actually a little ashamed both of Earl's Court and of himself.

"What!" he said; "you want to make a builder of model cottages of me, do you?" And he positively put his own hand upon the childish one and stroked it.

"Those must be pulled down," said Fauntleroy, with great eagerness. "Dearest says so. Let us—let us go and have them pulled down tomorrow. The people will be so glad when they see you! They'll know you have come to help them!" And his eyes shone like stars in his glowing face.

The Earl rose from his chair and put his hand on the child's shoulder. "Let us go out and take our walk on the terrace," he said, with a short laugh; "and we can talk it over."

And though he laughed two or three times again, as they walked to and fro on the broad stone terrace, where they walked together almost every fine evening, he seemed to be thinking of something which did not displease him, and still he kept his hand on his small companion's shoulder.

From *Little Lord Fauntleroy* (1886)

Grandmother's Spring

JULIANA HORATIA EWING

"In my young days," the grandmother said
       (Nodding her head,
Where cap and curls were as white as snow),
"In my young days when we used to go
       Rambling,
       Scrambling;
Each little dirty hand in hand,
Like a chain of daisies, a comical band
Of neighbours' children, seriously straying,
Really and truly going a-Maying,
My mother would bid us linger,
And lifting a slender, straight forefinger,
       Would say—
'Little Kings and Queens of the May,
       Listen to me!
       If you want to be
Every one of you very good
In that beautiful, beautiful, beautiful wood,

Where the little birds' heads get so turned with delight,
That some of them sing all night:
>> Whatever you pluck,
>> Leave some for good luck;
Picked from the stalk, or pulled up by the root,
From overhead or from underfoot,
Water-wonders of pond or brook;
>> Wherever you look,
>> And whatever you find—
>> Leave something behind:
>> Some for the Naiads,
>> Some for the Dryads,
And a bit for the Nixies, and the Pixies.'"

"After all these years," the grandame said,
>> Lifting her head,
"I think I can hear my mother's voice
>> Above all other noise,
Saying, 'Hearken, my child!
There is nothing more destructive and wild,
No wild bull with his horns,
No wild briar with clutching thorns,
No pig that routs in your garden-bed,
No robber with ruthless tread,
>> More reckless and rude
And wasteful of all things lovely and good,
Than a child with the face of a boy and the ways of a bear,
>> Who *doesn't care:*
Or some little ignorant minx
>> Who *never thinks.*
Now I never knew so stupid an elf
That he couldn't think and care for himself.
Oh, little sisters and little brothers,

Think for others, and care for others!
And of all that your little fingers find,
         Leave something behind,
For love of those that come after:
Some, perchance, to cool tired eyes in the moss that stifled
     your laughter!
             Pluck, children, pluck!
             But leave—for good luck—
             Some for the Naiads,
             And some for the Dryads,
And a bit for the Nixies, and the Pixies.'"

     .   .   .   .   .   .

"I was but a maid," the grandame said,
"When my mother was dead;
And many a time have I stood
In that beautiful wood,
To dream that through every woodland noise,
             Through the cracking
             Of twigs and the bending of bracken,
             Through the rustling
Of leaves in the breeze,
             And the bustling
Of dark-eyed, tawny-tailed squirrels flitting about the trees,
Through the purling and trickling cool
Of the streamlet that feeds the pool,
             I could hear her voice.
Should I wonder to hear it? Why?
Are the voices of tender wisdom apt to die?
And now, though I'm very old,

And the air, that used to feel fresh, strikes chilly and cold,
              On a sunny day when I potter
              About the garden, or totter
To the seat from where I can see, below,
The marsh and the meadow I used to know,
Bright with the bloom of the flowers that blossomed there
    long ago:
              Then, as if it were yesterday,
              I fancy I hear them say—
              'Pluck, children, pluck,
              But leave some for good luck:
Picked from the stalk, or pulled up by the root,

From overhead, or from underfoot,
Water-wonders of pond or brook;
Wherever you look
       And whatever your little fingers find,
       Leave something behind:
       Some for the Naiads,
       And some for the Dryads,
And a bit for the Nixies, and the Pixies.'"

From Verses for Children (1895)

The Little Creature

WALTER DE LA MARE

Twinkum, twankum, twirlum and twitch—
My great grandam—She was a Witch.
Mouse in wainscot Saint in niche—
My great grandam—She was a Witch:
Deadly nightshade flowers in a ditch—
My great grandam—She was a Witch;
Long though the shroud, it grows stitch by stitch—
My great grandam—She was a Witch;
Wean your weakling before you breech—
My great grandam—She was a Witch;
The fattest pig's but a double flitch—
My great grandam—She was a Witch;
Nightjars rattle, owls scritch—
My great grandam—She was a Witch.

Pretty and small,
A mere nothing at all,
Pinned up sharp in the ghost of a shawl,
She'd straddle her down to the kirkyard wall,

45

And mutter and whisper and call,
And call . . .

Red blood out and black blood in,
My Nannie says I'm a child of sin.
How did I choose me my witchcraft kin?
Know I as soon as dark's dreams begin
Snared is my heart in a nightmare's gin;
Never from terror I out may win;
So dawn and dusk I pine, peak, thin,
Scarcely knowing t'other from which—
My great grandam—She was a Witch.

From *Complete Poems*

Cousin Helen's Visit

SUSAN COOLIDGE

Katy has been a popular girl for a century, for she first appeared in her native America in 1872. What Katy Did *was followed by* What Katy Did At School, What Katy Did Next, *and other titles.*

A little knot of the school-girls were walking home together one afternoon in July. As they neared Dr. Carr's gate, Maria Fiske exclaimed, at the sight of a pretty bunch of flowers lying in the middle of the sidewalk:

"Oh my!" she cried, "see what somebody's dropped! I'm going to have it." She stooped to pick it up. But, just as her fingers touched the stems, the nosegay, as if bewitched, began to move. Maria made a bewildered clutch. The nosegay moved faster, and at last vanished under the gate, while a giggle sounded from the other side of the hedge.

"Did you see that?" shrieked Maria; "those flowers ran away of themselves."

"Nonsense," said Katy, "it's those absurd children." Then, opening the gate, she called: "John! Dorry! come out and show yourselves." But nobody replied, and no one could be seen. The nosegay lay on the path, however, and picking it

47

up, Katy exhibited to the girls a long end of black thread, tied to the stems.

"That's a very favourite trick of Johnnie's," she said; "he and Dorry are always tying up flowers, and putting them out on the walk to tease people. Here, Maria, take them if you like. Though I don't think John's taste in bouquets is very good."

"Isn't it splendid to have vacation come?" said one of the bigger girls. "What are you all going to do? We're going to the sea-side."

"Papa says he'll take Susie and me to Niagara," said Maria.

"I'm going to pay my aunt a visit," said Alice Blair. "She lives in a really lovely place in the country, and there's a pond there; and Tom (that's my cousin) says he'll teach me to row. What are you going to do, Katy?"

"Oh, I don't know; play about and have splendid times," replied Katy, throwing her bag of books into the air, and catching it again. But the other girls looked as if they didn't think this good fun at all, and as if they were sorry for her; and Katy felt suddenly that her vacation wasn't going to be so pleasant as that of the rest.

"I wish papa *would* take us somewhere," she said to Clover, as they walked up the gravel path. "All the other girls' papas do."

"He's too busy," replied Clover. "Besides, I don't think any of the rest of the girls have half such good times as we. Ellen Robbins says she'd give a million of dollars for such nice brothers and sisters as ours to play with. And, you know, Maria and Susie have awful times at home, though they do go to places. Mrs. Fiske is so particular. She always says 'Don't', and they haven't got any yard to their house, or anything. I wouldn't change."

"Nor I," said Katy, cheering up at these words of wisdom. "Oh, isn't it lovely to think there won't be any school to-morrow? Vacations are just splendid!" and she gave her bag another toss. It fell to the ground with a crash.

"There, you've cracked your slate," said Clover.

"No matter, I shan't want it again for eight weeks," replied Katy, comfortably, as they ran up the steps.

They burst open the front door, and raced upstairs crying "Hurrah! hurrah! vacation's begun. Aunt Izzie, vacation's begun!" Then they stopped short, for lo! the upper hall was all in confusion. Sounds of beating and dusting came from the spare room. Tables and chairs were standing about; and a cot-bed, which seemed to be taking a walk all by itself, had stopped short at the head of the stairs, and barred the way.

"Why, how queer!" said Katy, trying to get past. "What *can* be going to happen? Oh, there's Aunt Izzie! Aunt Izzie, who's coming? What *are* you moving the things out of the Blue-room for?"

"Oh, gracious! is that you?" replied Aunt Izzie, who looked very hot and flurried. "Now, children, it's no use for you to stand there asking questions; I haven't got time to answer them. Let the bedstead alone, Katy, you'll push it into the wall. There, I told you so!" as Katy gave an impatient shove, "you've made a bad mark on the paper. What a troublesome child you are! Go right downstairs, both of you, and don't come up this way again till after tea. I've just as much as I can possibly attend to till then."

"Just tell us what's going to happen, and we will," cried the children.

"Your Cousin Helen is coming to visit us," said Miss Izzie, curtly, and disappeared into the Blue-room.

This was news indeed. Katy and Clover ran downstairs in great excitement, and after consulting a little, retired to the loft to talk it over in peace and quiet. Cousin Helen coming! It seemed as strange as if Queen Victoria, gold crown and all, had invited herself to tea. Or as if some character out of a book, Robinson Crusoe, say, or Amy Herbert, had driven up with a trunk, and announced the intention of spending a week. For to the imaginations of the children, Cousin Helen was as interesting and unreal as anybody in the Fairy Tales—Cinderella, or Blue-beard, or dear Red Riding-Hood herself. Only there was a sort of mixture of Sunday-school book in their idea of her, for Cousin Helen was very, very good.

None of them had ever seen her. Philly said he was sure she hadn't any legs, because she never went away from home, and lay on a sofa all the time. But the rest knew that this was because Cousin Helen was ill. Papa always went to visit her twice a year, and he liked to talk to the children about her, and tell how sweet and patient she was, and what a pretty room she lived in. Katy and Clover had "played Cousin Helen" so long, that now they were frightened as well as glad at the idea of seeing the real one.

"Do you suppose she will want us to say hymns to her *all* the time?" asked Clover.

"Not all the time," replied Katy, "because you know she'll get tired, and have to take naps in the afternoons. And then, of course, she reads the Bible a great deal. Oh dear, how quiet we shall have to be! I wonder how long she's going to stay?"

"What do you suppose she looks like?" went on Clover.

"Something like 'Lucy', in Mrs. Sherwood, I suppose, with blue eyes, and curls, and a long, straight nose. And she'll keep her hands clasped *so* all the time, and wear 'frilled wrappers', and lie on the sofa perfectly still, and never smile, but just look patient. We'll have to take off our boots in the hall, Clover, and go upstairs in stocking feet, so as not to make a noise, all the time she stays."

"Won't it be funny!" giggled Clover, her sober little face growing bright at the idea of this variation on the hymns.

The time seemed very long till the next afternoon, when Cousin Helen was expected. Aunt Izzie, who was in a great excitement, gave the children many orders about their behaviour. They were to do this and that, and not to do the other. Dorry, at last, announced that he wished Cousin Helen would just stay at home. Clover and Elsie, who had been thinking very much the same thing in private, were glad to hear that she was on her way to a water-cure, and would stay only four days.

Five o'clock came. They all sat on the steps waiting for the carriage. At last it drove up. Papa was on the box. He motioned the children to stand back. Then he helped out a nice-looking woman, who, Aunt Izzie told them, was Cousin Helen's nurse, and then, very carefully, lifted Cousin Helen in his arms and brought her in.

"Oh, there are the chicks!" were the first words the children heard, in *such* a gay, pleasant voice. "Do set me down somewhere, Uncle. I want to see them so much!"

So papa put Cousin Helen on the hall sofa. The nurse fetched a pillow, and when she was made comfortable, Dr. Carr called to the little ones.

"Cousin Helen wants to see you," he said.

"Indeed I do," said the bright voice. "So this is Katy? Why, what a splendid tall Katy it is! And this is Clover," kissing her; "and *this* dear little Elsie. You all look as natural as possible—just as if I had seen you before." And she hugged them all round, not as if it was polite to like them because they were relations, but as if she had loved them and wanted them all her life.

There was something in Cousin Helen's face and manner, which made the children at home with her at once. Even Philly, who had backed away with his hands behind him, after staring hard for a minute or two, came up with a sort of rush to get his share of kissing.

Still, Katy's first feeling was one of disappointment. Cousin Helen was not at all like "Lucy", in Mrs. Sherwood's story. Her nose turned up the least bit in the world. She had brown hair, which didn't curl, a brown skin, and bright eyes, which danced when she laughed or spoke. Her face was thin, but except for that you wouldn't have guessed that she was sick. She didn't fold her hands, and she didn't look patient, but absolutely glad and merry. Her dress wasn't a "frilled wrapper", but a sort of loose travelling thing of pretty grey stuff, with a rose-coloured bow, and bracelets, and a round hat trimmed with a grey feather. All Katy's dreams about the "saintly invalid" seemed to take wings and fly away. But the more she watched Cousin Helen the more she seemed to like her, and to feel as if she were nicer than the imaginary person which she and Clover had invented.

"She looks just like other people, doesn't she?" whispered Cecy, who had come over to have a peep at the new arrival.

"Y-e-s," replied Katy, doubtfully, "only a great, great deal prettier."

By and by, papa carried Cousin Helen upstairs. All the children wanted to go too, but he told them she was tired, and must rest. So they went outdoors to play till tea-time.

"Oh, do let me take up the tray," cried Katy at the tea-table, as she watched Aunt Izzie getting ready Cousin Helen's supper. Such a nice supper! Cold chicken, and raspberries and cream, and tea in a pretty pink-and-white china cup. And such a snow-white napkin as Aunt Izzie spread over the tray!

"No, indeed," said Aunt Izzie; "you'll drop it the first thing." But Katy's eyes begged so hard, that Dr. Carr said: "Yes, let her, Izzie; I like to see the girls useful."

So Katy, proud of the commission, took the tray and carried it carefully across the hall. There was a bowl of flowers on the table. As she passed, she was struck with a bright idea. She let down the tray, and picking out a rose, laid it on the napkin beside the saucer of crimson raspberries. It looked very pretty, and Katy smiled to herself with pleasure.

"What are you stopping for?" called Aunt Izzie, from the dining-room. "*Do* be careful, Katy. I really think Bridget had better take it."

"Oh, no, no!" protested Katy; "I'm almost up already." And she sped upstairs as fast as she could go. Luckless speed! She had just reached the door of the Blue-room, when she tripped upon her boot-lace, which, as usual, was dangling, made a misstep, and stumbled. She caught at the door to save herself; the door flew open; and Katy, with the tray, cream, raspberries, rose and all, descended in a confused heap upon the carpet.

"I told you so!" exclaimed Aunt Izzie from the bottom of the stairs.

Katy never forgot how kind Cousin Helen was on this occasion. She was in bed, and was of course a good deal startled at the sudden crash and tumble on her floor. But after one little jump, nothing could have been sweeter than the way in which she comforted poor crestfallen Katy, and made so merry over the accident, that even Aunt Izzie almost forgot to scold. The broken dishes were piled up and the carpet made clean again, while Aunt Izzie prepared another tray just as nice as the first.

"Please let Katy bring it up!" pleaded Cousin Helen, in

her pleasant voice; "I am sure she will be careful this time. And Katy, I want just such another rose on the napkin. That was your doing—wasn't it?"

Katy *was* careful; this time all went well. The tray was placed safely on a little table beside the bed, and Katy sat watching Cousin Helen eat her supper with a warm loving feeling at her heart. I think we are scarcely ever so grateful to people as when they help us to get back our own self-esteem.

Cousin Helen hadn't much appetite, though she declared everything was delicious. Katy could see that she was very tired.

"Now," she said, when she had finished, "if you'll shake up this pillow—*so*, and move this other pillow a little, I think I will settle myself to sleep. Thanks—that's just right. Why, Katy dear, you are a born nurse. Now kiss me. Good night! To-morrow we will have a nice talk."

Katy went downstairs very happy. "Cousin Helen's perfectly lovely," she told Clover. "And she's got on the most *beautiful* night-gown, all lace and ruffles. It's just like a night-gown in a book."

"Isn't it wicked to care about clothes when you're sick?" questioned Cecy.

"I don't believe Cousin Helen *could* do anything wicked," said Katy.

"I told mamma that she had on bracelets, and mamma said she feared your cousin was a worldly person," retorted Cecy, primming up her lips.

Katy and Clover were quite distressed at this opinion. They talked about it while they were undressing.

"I mean to ask Cousin Helen to-morrow," said Katy.

Next morning the children got up very early. They were so glad that it was vacation. If it hadn't been, they would have been forced to go to school without seeing Cousin Helen, for she didn't wake till late. They grew so impatient of the delay, and went upstairs so often to listen at the door, and see if she were moving, that Aunt Izzie finally had to order them off. Katy rebelled against this order a good deal, but she consoled herself by going into the garden and picking the prettiest flowers she could find to give to Cousin Helen the moment she should see her.

When Aunt Izzie let her go up, Cousin Helen was lying

on the sofa all dressed for the day in a fresh blue muslin, with blue ribbons, and pretty bronze slippers with rosettes on the toes. The sofa had been wheeled round with its back to the light. There was a cushion with a pretty fluted cover, that Katy had never seen before, and several other things were scattered about, which gave the room quite a different air. All the house was neat, but somehow Aunt Izzie's rooms never were *pretty*. Children's eyes are quick to perceive such things, and Katy saw at once that the Blue-room had never looked like this.

Cousin Helen was white and tired, but her eyes and smile were as bright as ever. She was delighted with the flowers, which Katy presented rather shyly.

"Oh, how lovely!" she said; "I must put them in water immediately. Katy dear, won't you bring that little vase on the bureau and set it on this chair beside me? And please pour a little water into it first."

"What a beauty!" cried Katy, as she lifted the graceful white cup swung on a gilt stand. "Is it yours, Cousin Helen?"

"Yes, it is my pet vase. It stands on a little table beside me at home, and I fancied that the water-cure would seem more home-like if I had it with me there, so I brought it along. But why do you look so puzzled, Katy? Does it seem queer that a vase should travel about in a trunk?"

"No," said Katy slowly; "I was only thinking—Cousin Helen, is it worldly to have pretty things when you're sick?"

Cousin Helen laughed heartily.

"What put that idea into your head?" she asked.

"Cecy said so when I told her about your beautiful night-gown."

Cousin Helen laughed again.

"Well," she said, "I'll tell you what I think, Katy. Pretty things are no more 'worldly' than ugly ones, except when they spoil us by making us vain, or careless of the comfort of other people. And sickness is such a disagreeable thing in itself, that unless sick people take great pains, they soon grow to be eyesores to themselves and everybody about them. I don't think it is possible for an invalid to be too particular. And when one has the back-ache, and the head-ache, and the all-over-ache," she added, smiling, "there isn't much danger of growing vain because of a ruffle more or less on one's night-gown or a bit of bright ribbon."

Then she began to arrange the flowers, touching each separate one gently, and as if she loved it.

"What a queer noise!" she exclaimed, suddenly stopping.

It *was* queer—a sort of snuffling and snorting sound, as if a walrus or a sea-horse were promenading up and down in the hall. Katy opened the door. Behold! there were John and Dorry, very red in the face from flattening their noses against the key-hole, in a vain attempt to see if Cousin Helen were up and ready to receive company.

"Oh, let them come in!" cried Cousin Helen from her sofa.

So they came in, followed, before long, by Clover and Elsie. Such a merry morning as they had! Cousin Helen proved to possess a perfect genius for story-telling, and for suggesting games which could be played about her sofa, and did not make more noise than she could bear. Aunt Izzie, dropping in about eleven o'clock, found them having such a good time, that almost before she knew it, *she* was drawn into the game too. Nobody had ever heard of such a thing before! There sat Aunt Izzie on the floor, with three long lamp-lighters stuck in her hair, playing, "I'm a genteel lady, always genteel", in the jolliest manner possible. The children were so enchanted at the spectacle that they could hardly attend to the game, and were always forgetting how many "horns" they had. Clover privately thought that Cousin Helen must be a witch; and papa, when he came home at noon, said almost the same thing.

"What have you been doing to them, Helen?" he inquired, as he opened the door and saw the merry circle on the carpet. Aunt Izzie's hair was half pulled down, and Philly was rolling over and over in convulsions of laughter. But Cousin Helen said she hadn't done anything, and pretty soon papa was on the floor too, playing away as fast as the rest.

"I must put a stop to this," he cried, when everybody was tired of laughing, and everybody's head was stuck as full of paper quills as a porcupine's back. "Cousin Helen will be worn out. Run away, all of you, and don't come near this door again till the clock strikes four. Do you hear, chicks? Run—run! Shoo! shoo!"

The children scuttled away like a brood of fowls—all but Katy. "Oh, Papa, I'll be *so* quiet!" she pleaded. "Mightn't I stay just till the dinner-bell rings?"

"Do let her!" said Cousin Helen. So papa said, "Yes."

Katy sat on the floor, holding Cousin Helen's hand, and listening to her talk with papa. It interested her, though it was about things and people she did not know.

"How is Alex?" asked Dr. Carr at length.

"Quite well now," replied Cousin Helen, with one of her brightest looks. "He was run down and tired in the spring, and we were a little anxious about him, but Emma persuaded him to take a fortnight's vacation, and he came back all right."

"Do you see them often?"

"Almost every day. And little Helen comes every day, you know, for her lessons."

"Is she as pretty as she used to be?"

"Oh, yes—prettier, I think. She is a lovely little creature. Having her so much with me is one of my greatest treats.

Alex tries to think that she looks a little as I used to. But that is a compliment so great that I dare not appropriate it."

Dr. Carr stooped and kissed Cousin Helen as if he could not help it. "My *dear* child," he said. That was all; but something in the tone made Katy curious.

"Papa," she said, after dinner, "who is Alex that you and Cousin Helen were talking about?"

"Why, Katy? What makes you want to know?"

"I can't exactly tell—only Cousin Helen looked so;—and you kissed her;—and I thought perhaps it was something interesting."

"So it is," said Dr. Carr, drawing her on to his knee. "I've a mind to tell you about it, Katy, because you're old enough to see how beautiful it is, and wise enough, I hope, not to chatter or ask questions. Alex is the name of somebody, who, long ago, when Cousin Helen was well and strong, she loved, and expected to marry."

"Oh! why didn't she?" cried Katy.

"She met with a dreadful accident," continued Dr. Carr. "For a long time they thought she would die. Then she grew slowly better, and the doctors told her that she might live a good many years, but that she would have to lie on her sofa always, and be helpless and a cripple.

"Alex felt dreadfully when he heard this. He wanted to marry Cousin Helen just the same, and be her nurse, and take care of her always; but she would not consent. She broke the engagement, and told him that some day she hoped he would love somebody else well enough to marry her. So, after a good many years, he did, and now he and his wife live next door to Cousin Helen, and are her dearest friends. Their little girl is named 'Helen'. All their plans are talked over with her, and there is nobody in the world they think so much of."

"But doesn't it make Cousin Helen feel bad when she sees them walking about and enjoying themselves, and she can't move?" asked Katy.

"No," said Dr. Carr, "it doesn't; because Cousin Helen is half an angel already, and loves other people better than herself. I'm very glad she could come here for once. She's an example to us all, Katy, and I couldn't ask anything better than to have my little girls take pattern after her."

"It must be *awful* to be ill," soliloquized Katy, after papa was gone. "Why, if I had to stay in bed a whole week—I should *die*, I know I should."

Poor Katy! It seemed to her, as it does to almost all young people, that there is nothing in the world so easy as to die, the moment things go wrong!

This conversation with papa made Cousin Helen doubly interesting in Katy's eyes. "It was just like something in a book," to be in the same house with the heroine of a love story so sad and sweet.

The play that afternoon was much interrupted, for every few minutes somebody had to run in and see if it wasn't four o'clock. The instant the hour came, all six children galloped upstairs.

"I think we'll tell stories this time," said Cousin Helen.

So they told stories. Cousin Helen's were the best of all. There was one of them about a robber, which sent delightful chills creeping down all their backs. All but Philly. He was so excited that he grew warlike.

"I ain't afraid of robbers," he declared, strutting up and down. "When they come, I shall just cut them in two with my sword which papa gave me. They did come once. I did cut them in two—three, five, eleven of 'em. You'll see!"

But that evening, after the younger children were gone to bed, and Katy and Clover were sitting in the Blue-room, a lamentable howling was heard from the nursery. Clover ran to see what was the matter. Behold—there was Phil, sitting up in bed, and crying for help.

"There's robbers under the bed," he sobbed; "ever so many robbers."

"Why, no, Philly!" said Clover, peeping under the valance to satisfy him; "there isn't anybody there."

"Yes, there is, I tell you," declared Phil, holding her tight. "I heard one. They were *chewing* my over-shoes."

"Poor little fellow!" said Cousin Helen, when Clover, having pacified Phil, came back to report. "It's a warning against robber stories. But this one ended so well, that I didn't think of anybody's being frightened."

It was no use, after this, for Aunt Izzie to make rules about going into the Blue-room. She might as well have ordered flies to keep away from a sugar-bowl. By hook or by crook, the children *would* get upstairs. Whenever Aunt Izzie went in, she was sure to find them there, just as close to Cousin Helen as they could get. And Cousin Helen begged her not to interfere.

"We have only three or four days to be together," she said. "Let them come as much as they like. It won't hurt me a bit."

Little Elsie clung with a passionate love to this new friend. Cousin Helen had sharp eyes. She saw the wistful look in Elsie's face at once, and took special pains to be sweet and tender to her. This preference made Katy jealous. She couldn't bear to share her cousin with anybody.

When the last evening came, and they went up after tea to the Blue-room, Cousin Helen was opening a box which had just come by Express.

"It is a Good-bye Box," she said. "All of you must sit down in a row, and when I hide my hands behind me, *so*, you must choose in turn which you will take."

So they all chose in turn, "Which hand will you have, the right or the left?" and Cousin Helen, with the air of a wise fairy, brought out from behind her pillow something pretty for each one. First came a vase exactly like her own, which Katy had admired so much. Katy screamed with delight as it was placed in her hands:

"Oh, how lovely! how lovely!" she cried. "I'll keep it as long as I live and breathe."

"If you do, it'll be the first time you ever kept anything for a week without breaking it," remarked Aunt Izzie.

Next came a pretty purple pocket-book for Clover. It was just what she wanted, for she had lost her portemonnaie. Then a sweet little locket on a bit of velvet ribbon, which Cousin Helen tied round Elsie's neck.

"There's a piece of my hair in it," she said. "Why, Elsie, darling, what's the matter? Don't cry so!"

"Oh, you're s-o beautiful and s-o sweet!" sobbed Elsie; "and you're go-o-ing away."

Dorry had a box of dominoes, and John a solitaire board. For Phil there appeared a book—*The History of the Robber Cat.*

"That will remind you of the night when the thieves came and chewed your over-shoes," said Cousin Helen, with a mischievous smile. They all laughed, Phil loudest of all.

Nobody was forgotten. There was a notebook for papa, and a set of ivory tablets for Aunt Izzie. Even Cecy was remembered. Her present was *The Book of Golden Deeds*, with all sorts of stories about boys and girls who had done brave and good things. She was almost too pleased to speak.

"Oh, thank you, Cousin Helen!" she said at last. Cecy wasn't a cousin, but she and the Carr children were in the habit of sharing their aunts and uncles, and relations generally, as they did their other good things.

Next day came the sad parting. All the little ones stood at the gate, to wave their pocket-handkerchiefs as the carriage drove away. When it was quite out of sight, Katy rushed off to "weep a little weep", all by herself.

"Papa said he wished we were all like Cousin Helen," she thought, as she wiped her eyes, "and I mean to try, though I don't suppose if I tried a thousand years I should ever get to be half so good. I'll study, and keep my things in order, and be ever so kind to the little ones. Dear me—if only Aunt Izzie was Cousin Helen, how easy it would be! Never mind—I'll think about her all the time, and I'll begin to-morrow."

From *What Katy Did* (1872)

Jo Meets Apollyon

LOUISA MAY ALCOTT

I have chosen this chapter for a personal reason, even though it shows the famous Marches in one of their less happy moments. It may sound a shade pious, but it contains a valuable bit of advice that I have remembered with almost annoying vividness since I was eight years old and found the book stuffed away in the bottom of a cupboard in my grandmother's house. I still try to hang on to it grimly at appropriate moments—it's the bit about not letting the sun go down on your anger.

"Girls, where are you going?" asked Amy, coming into their room one Saturday afternoon, and finding them getting ready to go out, with an air of secrecy, which excited her curiosity.

"Never mind; girls shouldn't ask questions," returned Jo.

Now if there *is* anything mortifying to our feelings when we are young, it is to be told that; and to be bidden to "run away, dear," is still more trying to us. Amy bridled up at this insult, and determined to find out the secret, if she teased for an hour. Turning to Meg, who never refused her anything very long, she said coaxingly, "Do tell me! I should think you might let me go too, for Beth is fussing over her piano, and I haven't got anything to do, and am *so* lonely."

"I can't, dear, because you aren't invited," began Meg; but Jo broke in impatiently, "Now, Meg, be quiet, or you will spoil it all. You can't go, Amy, so don't be a baby and whine."

"You are going somewhere with Laurie, I know you are; you were whispering together, on the sofa, last night, and you stopped when I came in. Aren't you going with him?"

"Yes, we are; now do be still and stop bothering."

Amy saw Meg slip a fan into her pocket.

"I know! I know! you're going to the hall to see the *Seven Castles!*" she cried, adding resolutely, "and I *shall* go, for mother said I might see it; and I've got my rag-money, and it was mean not to tell me in time,"

"Just listen to me a minute, and be a good child," said Meg, soothingly. "Mother doesn't wish you to go this week, because your eyes are not well enough yet to bear the light. Next week you can go with Beth and Hannah, and have a nice time."

"I don't like that half as well as going with you and Laurie. Please let me; I've been sick with this cold so long, and shut up, I'm dying for some fun. Do, Meg! I'll be ever so good," pleaded Amy, looking as pathetic as she could.

"Suppose we take her. I don't believe mother would mind, if we bundle her up well," began Meg.

"If *she* goes *I* shan't; and if I don't, Laurie won't like it; and it will be very rude, after he invited only us, to go and drag in Amy. I should think she'd hate to poke herself where she isn't wanted," said Jo, crossly, for she disliked the trouble of overseeing a fidgety child, when she wanted to enjoy herself.

Her tone and manner angered Amy, who began to put her boots on, saying, in her most aggravating way, "I *shall* go; Meg says I may; and if I pay for myself, Laurie hasn't anything to do with it."

"You can't sit with us, for our seats are reserved, and you mustn't sit alone; so Laurie will give you his place, and that will spoil our pleasure; or he'll get another seat for you, and that isn't proper, when you weren't asked. You shan't stir a step; so you may just stay where you are," scolded Jo, crosser than ever, having just pricked her finger in her hurry.

Sitting on the floor, with one boot on, Amy began to cry, and Meg to reason with her, when Laurie called from below and the two girls hurried down, leaving their sister wailing; for now and then she forgot her grown-up ways, and acted like a spoilt child. Just as the party were setting out, Amy called over the banisters, in a threatening tone, "You'll be sorry for this, Jo March; see if you ain't."

"Fiddlesticks!" returned Jo, slamming the door.

They had a charming time, for *The Seven Castles of the Diamond Lake* was as brilliant and wonderful as heart could wish. But, in spite of the comical red imps, sparkling elves, and gorgeous princes and princesses, Jo's pleasure had a drop of bitterness in it; the fairy queen's yellow curls reminded her of Amy; and between the acts she amused herself with wondering what her sister would do to make her "sorry for it." She and Amy had had many lively skirmishes in the course of their lives, for both had quick tempers, and were apt to be violent when fairly roused. Amy teased Jo, and Jo irritated Amy, and semi-occasional explosions occurred, of which both were much ashamed afterwards. Although the oldest, Jo had the least self-control, and had hard times trying to curb the fiery spirit which was continually getting her into trouble; her anger never lasted long, and having humbly confessed her fault she sincerely repented and tried to do better. Her sisters used to say that they rather liked to get Jo into a fury because she was such an angel afterwards.

Poor Jo tried desperately to be good, but her bosom enemy was always ready to flame up and defeat her; and it took years of patient effort to subdue it.

When they got home they found Amy reading in the parlour. She assumed an injured air as they came in; never lifted her eyes from her book, or asked a single question. Perhaps curiosity might have conquered resentment, if Beth had not been there to inquire, and receive a glowing description of the play. On going up to put away her best hat, Jo's first look was towards the bureau; for in their last quarrel, Amy had soothed her feelings by turning Jo's top drawer upside down on the floor. Everything was in its place, however, and after a hasty glance into her various closets, bags and boxes, Jo decided that Amy had forgiven and forgotten her wrongs.

There Jo was mistaken; for next day she made a discovery which produced a tempest. Meg, Beth and Amy were sitting together, late in the afternoon, when Jo burst into the room, looking excited and demanding breathlessly. "Has anyone taken my book?"

Meg and Beth said "No" at once, and looked surprised; Amy poked the fire, and said nothing. Jo saw her colour rise, and was down upon her in a minute.

"Amy, you've got it."

"No, I haven't."

"You know where it is, then!"

"No, I don't."

"That's a fib!" cried Jo, taking her by the shoulders and looking fiercely enough to frighten a braver child than Amy.

"It isn't. I haven't got it, don't know where it is now, and don't care."

"You know something about it, and you'd better tell at once, or I'll make you," and Jo gave her a slight shake.

"Scold as much as you like, you'll never see your silly old book again," cried Amy, getting excited in her turn.

"Why not?"

"I burnt it up!"

"What! My little book I was so fond of, and worked over, and meant to finish before father got home? Have you really burnt it?" said Jo, turning very pale, while her eyes kindled and her hands clutched Amy nervously.

"Yes! I did! I told you I'd make you pay for being so cross yesterday, and I have, so—"

Amy got no farther, for Jo's hot temper mastered her, and she shook Amy till her teeth chattered in her head; crying in a passion of grief and anger—

"You wicked, wicked girl! I never can write it again and I'll never forgive you as long as I live."

Meg flew to rescue Amy, and Beth to pacify Jo, but Jo was quite beside herself; and with a parting box on her sister's ear, she rushed out of the room up to the old sofa in the garret, and finished her fight alone.

The storm cleared up below, for Mrs March came home, and, having heard the story, soon brought Amy to a sense of the wrong she had done her sister. Jo's book was the pride of her heart, and was regarded by her family as a literary sprout of great promise. It was only half-a-dozen little fairy tales, but Jo had worked over them patiently, putting her whole heart into her work, hoping to make something good enough to print. She had just copied them with great care, and had destroyed the old manuscript, so that Amy's bonfire had consumed the loving work of several years. It seemed a small loss to others, but to Jo it was a dreadful calamity, and she felt it never could be made up to her. Beth mourned as for a departed kitten, and Meg refused to defend her pet; Mrs March looked grave and grieved, and Amy felt that no one would love her till she had asked pardon for the act which she now regretted more than any of them.

When the tea-bell rang Jo appeared, looking so grim and unapproachable, that it took all Amy's courage to say meekly—

"Please forgive me, Jo; I'm very, very sorry."

"I shall never forgive you," was Jo's stern reply; and from that moment she ignored Amy entirely.

No one spoke of the great trouble—not even Mrs March—for all had learned by experience that when Jo was in that mood words were wasted; and the wisest course was to wait till some little accident, or her own generous nature, softened Jo's resentment, and healed the breach. It was not a happy evening; for though they sewed as usual, while their mother read aloud from Bremer, Scott or Edgeworth, something was wanting, and the sweet home peace was disturbed. They felt this most when singing time came; for Beth could only play, Jo stood dumb as a stone, and Amy broke down, so Meg and Mother sang alone. But in spite of their efforts to be as cheery as larks, the flute-like voices did not seem to chord as well as usual, and all felt out of tune.

As Jo received her good-night kiss, Mrs March whispered gently—"My dear, don't let the sun go down upon your anger; forgive each other, help each other, and begin again tomorrow."

Jo wanted to lay her head down on that motherly bosom, and cry her grief and anger all away, but tears were an unmanly weakness, and she felt so deeply injured that she really *couldn't* quite forgive yet. So she winked hard, shook her head, and said gruffly, because Amy was listening—"It was an abominable thing, and she don't deserve to be forgiven."

With that she marched off to bed, and there was no merry or confidential gossip that night.

Amy was much offended that her overtures of peace had been repulsed, and began to wish she had not humbled herself, to feel more injured than ever, and to plume herself on her superior virtue in a way which was particularly exasperating. Jo still looked like a thundercloud, and nothing went well all day. It was bitter cold in the morning, she dropped her precious turnover in the gutter, Aunt March had an attack of fidgets, Meg was pensive, Beth *would* look grieved and wistful when she got home, and Amy kept making remarks about people who were always talking about being good, and yet wouldn't try, when other people set them a virtuous example.

"Everybody is so hateful, I'll ask Laurie to go skating. He is always so kind and jolly and will put me to rights, I know," said Jo to herself, and off she went.

Amy heard the clash of skates, and looked out with an impatient exclamation,—"There! She promised I should go next time, for this is the last ice we shall have. But it's no use to ask such a crosspatch to take me."

"Don't say that; you *were* very naughty, and it *is* hard to forgive the loss of her precious little book; but I think she might do it now, and I guess she will, if you try her at the right moment," said Meg. "Go after them; don't say anything until Jo has got good-natured with Laurie, then take a quiet minute, and just kiss her, and do some kind thing, and I'm sure she'll be friends again with all her heart."

"I'll try," said Amy, for the advice suited her; and after a flurry to get ready, she ran after the friends, who were just disappearing over the hill.

It was not far to the river, but both were ready before Amy reached them. Jo saw her coming and turned her back; Laurie did not see, for he was carefully skating along the shore, sounding the ice, for a warm spell had preceded the cold snap.

"I'll go on to the first bend and see if it's all right, before we begin to race," Amy heard him say, as he shot away, looking like a young Russian in his fur-trimmed coat and cap.

Jo heard Amy panting after her run, stamping her feet and blowing her fingers, as she tried to put her skates on; but Jo never turned, and went slowly zig-zagging down the river, taking a bitter, unhappy sort of satisfaction in her sister's troubles. She had cherished her anger till it grew strong, and took possession of her, as evil thoughts and feelings always do, unless cast out at once. As Laurie turned the bend, he shouted back—"Keep near the shore, it isn't safe in the middle."

Jo heard, but Amy was just struggling to her feet, and did not catch a word. Jo glanced over her shoulder and the little demon she was harbouring said in her ear— "No matter whether she heard or not, let her take care of herself."

Laurie had vanished round the bend; Jo was just at the turn, and Amy, far behind, striking out towards the smoother ice in the middle of the river. For a minute Jo stood still, with a strange feeling in her heart; then she resolved to go on, but something held and turned her round, just in time to see Amy throw up her hands and go down, with a sudden crash of rotten ice, the splash of water, and a cry that made Jo's heart stand still with fear. She tried to call Laurie, but her voice was gone; she tried to rush forward, but her feet seemed to have no strength in them; and, for a second, she could only stand motionless, staring, with a terror-stricken face, at the little blue hood above the black water. Something rushed swiftly by her, and Laurie's voice cried out—"Bring a rail; quick, quick!"

How she did it, she never knew; but for the next few minutes she worked as if possessed, blindly obeying Laurie, who was quite self-possessed, and, lying flat, held Amy up by his arm and hockey stick till Jo dragged a rail from the fence, and together they got the child out, more frightened than hurt.

"Now we must walk her home as fast as we can; pile our things on her, while I get off these confounded skates," cried Laurie, wrapping his coat round Amy, and tugging away at the straps, which never seemed so intricate before.

Shivering, dripping and crying, they got Amy home; and after an exciting time of it, she fell asleep, rolled in blankets, before a hot fire. During the bustle Jo had scarcely spoken, but flown about looking pale and wild, with her things half off, her dress torn, and her hands cut and bruised by ice and rails and refractory buckles. When Amy was comfortably asleep, and the house quiet, and Mrs March sitting by the bed, she called Jo to her, and began to bind up the hurt hands.

"Are you sure she is safe?" whispered Jo, looking remorsefully at the golden head, which might have been swept away from her sight for ever under the treacherous ice.

"Quite safe, dear; she is not hurt, and won't even take cold, I think, you were so sensible in covering and getting her home quickly," replied her mother, cheerfully.

"Laurie did it all; I only let her go. Mother, if she *should* die, it would be my fault"; and Jo dropped down beside the bed, in a passion of penitent tears, telling all that had happened, bitterly condemning her hardness of heart, and sobbing out her gratitude for being spared the heavy punishment which might have come upon her.

"It's my dreadful temper! I try to cure it; I think I have, and then it breaks out worse than ever. Oh, mother, what shall I do? what shall I do?" cried poor Jo, in despair.

"Watch and pray, dear; never get tired of trying; and never think it is impossible to conquer your fault," said Mrs March, kissing the wet cheek so tenderly that Jo cried harder than ever.

"You don't know, and you can't guess how bad it is! It seems as if I could do anything when I'm in a passion; I get so savage I could hurt anyone, and enjoy it. I'm afraid I *shall* do something dreadful some day, and spoil my life, and make everybody hate me. Oh, mother, help me, do help me!"

"I will, my child, I will. Don't cry so bitterly, but remember this day, and resolve, with all your soul, that you will never know another like it. Jo, dear, we all have our temptations, some far greater than yours, and it often takes us all our lives to conquer them. You think your temper is the worst in the world; but mine used to be just like it."

"Yours, mother? Why, you are never angry!" and, for the moment, Jo forgot remorse in surprise.

"I've been trying to cure it for forty years, and have only succeeded in controlling it. I am angry nearly every day of my life, Jo; but I have learned not to show it."

The patience and the humility of the face she loved so well was a better lesson to Jo than the wisest lecture, the sharpest reproof. She felt comforted at once by the sympathy and the confidence given her; the knowledge that her mother had a fault like hers, and tried to mend it, made her own easier to bear and strengthened her resolution to cure it; though forty years seemed rather a long time to watch and pray, to a girl of fifteen. . . .

From *Little Women* (1868)

The Burial of the Linnet

JULIANA HORATIA EWING

Found in the garden—dead in his beauty,
  Ah! that a linnet should die in the spring!
Bury him, comrades, in pitiful duty,
  Muffle the dinner-bell, solemnly ring.

Bury him kindly—up in the corner:
  Bird, beast and goldfish are sepulchred there;
Bid the black kitten march as chief mourner,
  Waving her tail like a plume in the air.

Bury him nobly—next to the donkey;
  Fetch the old banner, and wave it about;
Bury him deeply—think of the monkey,
  Shallow his grave, and the dogs got him out.

Bury him softly—white wool around him,
  Kiss his poor feathers,—the first kiss and last;
Tell his poor widow kind friends have found him:
  Plant his poor grave with whatever grows fast.

Farewell, sweet singer! dead in thy beauty,
  Silent through summer, though other birds sing;
Bury him, comrades, in pitiful duty,
  Muffle the dinner-bell, mournfully ring.

From *Verses for Children* (1895)

The Bennet Family

JANE AUSTEN

"What a fine thing for our girls!" *cries Mrs. Bennet, when she learns that an eligible bachelor, Mr. Bingley, has taken up residence nearby. She urges her husband to call on the newcomer without delay, but he tantalizes her by refusing to be pinned down.* "... I will send a few lines by you," *he tells her,* "to assure him of my hearty consent to his marrying whichever he chooses of the girls; though I must throw in a good word for my little Lizzy."

"I desire you will do no such thing. Lizzy is not a bit better than the others; and I am sure she is not half so handsome as Jane, nor half so good-humoured as Lydia. But you are always giving *her* the preference."

"They have none of them much to recommend them," replied he—"they are all silly and ignorant like other girls ..."

Mr Bennet (*explains Jane Austen*) was so odd a mixture of quick parts, sarcastic humour, reserve, and caprice, that the experience of three-and-twenty years had been insufficient to make his wife understand his character. *Her* mind was less difficult to develop. She was a woman of mean under-standing, little information, and uncertain temper. When she was discontented, she fancied herself nervous. The business of her life was to get her daughters married; its solace was visiting and news. . . .

This is Chapter II of the story:

Mr Bennet was among the earliest of those who waited on Mr Bingley. He had always intended to visit him, though to the last always assuring his wife that he should not go; and till the evening after the visit was paid she had no knowledge of it. It was then disclosed in the following manner. Observing his second daughter engaged in trimming a hat, he suddenly addressed her with,—

"I hope Mr Bingley will like it, Lizzy."

"We are not in a way to know *what* Mr Bingley likes," said her mother resentfully, "since we are not to visit."

"But you forget, mamma," said Elizabeth, "that we shall meet him at the assemblies, and that Mrs Long has promised to introduce him."

"I do not believe Mrs Long will do any such thing. She has two nieces of her own. She is a selfish, hypocritical woman, and I have no opinion of her."

"No more have I," said Mr Bennet; "and I am glad to find that you do not depend on her serving you."

Mrs Bennet deigned not to make any reply; but, unable to contain herself, began scolding one of her daughters.

"Don't keep coughing so, Kitty, for Heaven's sake! Have a little compassion on my nerves. You tear them to pieces."

"Kitty has no discretion in her coughs," said her father; "she times them ill."

"I do not cough for my own amusement," replied Kitty, fretfully.—"When is your next ball to be, Lizzy?"

"To-morrow fortnight."

"Ay, so it is," cried her mother. "And Mrs Long does not come back till the day before; so it will be impossible for her to introduce him, for she will not know him herself."

"Then, my dear, you may have the advantage of your friend, and introduce Mr Bingley to her."

"Impossible, Mr Bennet, impossible, when I am not acquainted with him myself; how can you be so teasing?"

"I honour your circumspection. A fortnight's acquaintance is certainly very little. One cannot know what a man really is by the end of a fortnight. But if *we* do not venture, somebody else will; and, after all, Mrs Long and her nieces must stand their chance, and therefore, as she will think it an act of kindness if you decline the office, I will take it on myself."

The girls stared at their father. Mrs Bennet said only,

"Nonsense, nonsense!"

"What can be the meaning of that emphatic exclamation?" cried he. "Do you consider the forms of introduction, and the stress that is laid on them, as nonsense? I cannot quite agree with you *there*.—What say you, Mary? For you are a young lady of deep reflection, I know, and read great books, and make extracts."

Mary wished to say something very sensible, but knew not how.

"While Mary is adjusting her ideas," he continued, "let us return to Mr Bingley."

"I am sick of Mr Bingley," cried his wife.

"I am sorry to hear *that*; but why did you not tell me so before? If I had known as much this morning, I certainly would not have called on him. It is very unlucky; but as I have actually paid the visit, we cannot escape the acquaintance now."

The astonishment of the ladies was just what he wished— that of Mrs Bennet perhaps surpassing the rest; though when the first tumult of joy was over, she began to declare that it was what she had expected all the while.

"How good it was in you, my dear Mr Bennet! But I knew I should persuade you at last. I was sure you loved your girls too well to neglect such an acquaintance. Well, how pleased I am! and it is such a good joke, too, that you should have gone this morning, and never said a word about it till now."

"Now, Kitty, you may cough as much as you choose," said Mr Bennet; and as he spoke he left the room, fatigued with the raptures of his wife.

"What an excellent father you have, girls!" said she, when the door was shut. "I do not know how you will ever make him amends for his kindness: or me either, for that matter. At our time of life it is not so pleasant, I can tell you, to be making new acquaintance every day; but for your sakes we would do anything.—Lydia, my love, though you *are* the youngest, I daresay Mr Bingley will dance with you at the next ball."

"Oh," said Lydia stoutly, "I am not afraid; for though I *am* the youngest, I'm the tallest."

The rest of the evening was spent in conjecturing how soon he would return Mr Bennet's visit, and determining when they should ask him to dinner.

From *Pride and Prejudice* (1813)

A Brother's Kind Thoughts for his Sisters

JANE AUSTEN

John Dashwood has inherited an estate and fortune from his father, who held it in trust for him. John has agreed to make provision for his father's widow, his second wife, and for her daughters—who are, of course, John's half-sisters. John's wife, Fanny, has her own ideas about this matter:

Mrs John Dashwood did not at all approve of what her husband intended to do for his sisters. To take three thousand pounds from the fortune of their dear little boy would be impoverishing him to the most dreadful degree. She begged him to think again on the subject. How could he answer it to himself to rob his child, and his only child, too, of so large a sum? And what possible claim could the Miss Dashwoods, who were related to him only by half blood, which she considered as no relationship at all, have on his generosity to so large an amount? It was very well known that no affection was ever supposed to exist between the children of any man by different marriages; and why was he to ruin himself, and their poor little Harry, by giving away all his money to his half-sisters?

"It was my father's last request to me," replied her husband, "that I should assist his widow and daughters."

"He did not know what he was talking of, I daresay; ten to one but he was light-headed at the time. Had he been in his right senses, he could not have thought of such a thing as begging you to give away half your fortune from your own child."

"He did not stipulate for any particular sum, my dear Fanny; he only requested me, in general terms, to assist them, and make their situation more comfortable than it was in his power to do. Perhaps it would have been as well if he had left it wholly to myself. He could hardly suppose I should neglect them. But as he required the promise, I could not do less than give it—at least I thought so at the time. The promise, therefore, was given and must be performed. Something must be done for them whenever they leave Norland and settle in a new home."

"Well, then, let something be done for them; but that something need not be three thousand pounds. Consider," she added, "that when the money is once parted with, it never can return. Your sisters will marry, and it will be gone for ever. If, indeed, it could ever be restored to our poor little boy—"

"Why, to be sure," said her husband, very gravely, "that would make a great difference. The time may come when Harry will regret that so large a sum was parted with. If he should have a numerous family, for instance, it would be a very convenient addition."

"To be sure it would."

"Perhaps, then, it would be better for all parties if the sum were diminished one half. Five hundred pounds would be a prodigious increase to their fortunes!"

"Oh! beyond anything great! What brother on earth

would do half so much for his sisters, even if *really* his sisters? And as it is—only half blood! But you have such a generous spirit!"

"I would not wish to do anything mean," he replied. "One had rather, on such occasions, do too much than too little. No one, at least, can think I have not done enough for them: even themselves, they can hardly expect more."

"There is no knowing what *they* may expect," said the lady; "but we are not to think of their expectations: the question is, what you can afford to do."

"Certainly; and I think I may afford to give them five hundred pounds apiece. As it is, without any addition of mine they will each have above three thousand pounds on their mother's death—a very comfortable fortune for any young woman."

"To be sure it is; and indeed it strikes me that they can want no addition at all. They will have ten thousand pounds divided among them. If they marry, they will be sure of doing well; and if they do not, they may all live very comfortably together on the interest of ten thousand pounds."

"That is very true, and, therefore, I do not know whether, upon the whole, it would not be more advisable to do something for their mother while she lives, rather than for them—something of the annuity kind, I mean. My sisters would feel the good effects of it as well as herself. A hundred a year would make them all perfectly comfortable."

His wife hesitated a little, however, in giving her consent to this plan.

"To be sure," said she, "it is better than parting with fifteen hundred pounds at once. But then, if Mrs Dashwood should live fifteen years, we shall be completely taken in."

"Fifteen years, my dear Fanny! Her life cannot be worth half that purchase!"

"Certainly not; but if you observe, people always live for ever when there is any annuity to be paid them; and she is very stout and healthy, and hardly forty. An annuity is a very serious business; it comes over and over every year, and there is no getting rid of it. You are not aware of what you are doing. I have known a great deal of the trouble of annuities; for my mother was clogged with the payment of three to old superannuated servants by my father's will, and it is amazing how disagreeable she found it. Twice every year these annuities were to be paid; and then there was the trouble of getting it to them; and then one of them was said to have died, and afterwards it turned out to be no such thing. My mother was quite sick of it. Her income was not her own, she said, with such perpetual claims on it; and it was the more unkind in my father, because, otherwise, the money would have been entirely at my mother's disposal, without any restriction whatever. It has given me such an abhorrence of annuities that I am sure I would not pin myself down to the payment of one for all the world."

"It is certainly an unpleasant thing," replied Mr Dashwood, "to have those kind of yearly drains on one's income. One's fortune, as your mother justly says, is *not* one's own. To be tied down to the regular payment of such a sum, on every rent-day, is by no means desirable: it takes away one's independence."

"Undoubtedly; and after all, you have no thanks for it. They think themselves secure; you do no more than what is expected, and it raises no gratitude at all. If I were you, whatever I did should be done at my own discretion entirely. I would not bind myself to allow them anything yearly. It may be very inconvenient some years to spare a hundred, or even fifty pounds, from our own expenses."

"I believe you are right, my love; it will be better that

there should be no annuity in the case. Whatever I give them occasionally will be of far greater assistance than a yearly allowance, because they would only enlarge their style of living if they felt sure of a larger income, and would not be sixpence the richer for it at the end of the year. It will certainly be much the best way. A present of fifty pounds now and then will prevent their ever being distressed for money, and will, I think, be amply discharging my promise to my father."

"To be sure it will. Indeed, to say truth, I am convinced within myself that your father had no idea of your giving them any money at all. The assistance he thought of, I dare-say, was only such as might be reasonably expected of you; for instance, such as looking out for a comfortable small house for them, helping them to move their things, and sending them presents of fish and game and so forth, whenever they are in season. I'll lay my life that he meant nothing further; indeed, it would be very strange and unreasonable if he did. Do but consider, my dear Mr Dashwood, how excessively comfortable your mother-in-law (*that is, stepmother. Ed.*) and her daughters may live on the interest of seven thousand pounds, besides the thousand pounds belonging to each of the girls, which brings them in fifty pounds a year apiece, and of course they will pay their mother for their board out of it. Altogether, they will have five hundred a year amongst them; and what on earth can four women want for more than that? They will live so cheap! Their housekeeping will be nothing at all. They will have no carriage, no horses, and hardly any servants; they will keep no company and can have no expenses of any kind. Only conceive how comfortable they will be! Five hundred a year! I am sure I cannot imagine how they will spend half of it; and as to your giving them more, it is quite absurd to think of it. They will be much more able to give *you* something."

"Upon my word," said Mr Dashwood, "I believe you are perfectly right. My father could certainly mean nothing more by his request to me than what you say. I clearly understand it now, and I will strictly fulfil my engagement by such acts of assistance and kindness to them as you have described. When my mother removes into another house, my services shall be readily given to accommodate her as far as I can. Some little present of furniture, too, may be acceptable then."

"Certainly," returned Mrs John Dashwood. "But, however, *one* thing must be considered. When your father and mother moved to Norland, though the furniture of Stanhill was sold, all the china, plate and linen was saved, and is now left to your mother. Her house will therefore be almost completely fitted up as soon as she takes it."

"That is a material consideration, undoubtedly, a valuable legacy, indeed! And yet some of the plate would have been a very pleasant addition to our own stock here."

"Yes; and the set of breakfast-china is twice as handsome as what belongs to this house; a great deal too handsome, in my opinion, for any place *they* can ever afford to live in. But, however, so it is. Your father thought only of *them.* And I must say this, that you owe no particular gratitude to him, nor attention to his wishes; for we very well know that if he could he would have left almost everything in the world to *them.*"

This argument was irresistible. It gave to his intentions whatever was wanting before; and he finally resolved that it would be absolutely unnecessary, if not highly indecorous, to do more for the widow and children of his father than such kind of neighbourly acts as his own wife pointed out.

From *Sense and Sensibility* (1811)

Two, Five and Seven

A Madrigal

ANON

Sister, awake! close not your eyes!
   The day her light discloses,
And the bright morning doth arise
   Out of her bed of roses.

See the clear sun, the world's bright eye,
   In at our window peeping:
Lo, how he blusheth to espy
   Us idle wenches sleeping!

Therefore awake! make haste, I say,
   And let us, without staying,
All in our gowns of green so gay
   Into the Park a-maying!

Thos. Bateson's First Set of English Madrigals (1604)

Five of Us

WALTER DE LA MARE

"Five of us small merry ones,
  And Simon in the grass.
  Here's an hour for delight,
  Out of mortal thought and sight.
  See, the sunshine ebbs away:
  We play and we play.

"Five of us small merry ones,
  And yonder there the stone,
  Flat and heavy, dark and cold,
  Where, beneath the churchyard mould,
  Time has buried yesterday:
  We play and we play.

"Five of us small merry ones,
  We sang a dirge, did we,
  Cloud was cold on foot and hair,
  And a magpie from her lair
  Spread her motley on the air;
  And we wept—our tears away:
  We play and we play."

From *Complete Poems*

We are Seven

WILLIAM WORDSWORTH

—A simple Child,
That lightly draws its breath,
And feels its life in every limb,
What should it know of death?

I saw a little cottage Girl:
She was eight years old, she said;
Her hair was thick with many a curl
That clustered round her head.

She had a rustic, woodland air,
And she was wildly clad:
Her eyes were fair, and very fair;
—Her beauty made me glad.

"Sisters and brothers, little maid,
How many may you be?"
"How many? Seven in all," she said,
And wondering looked at me.

"And where are they? I pray you tell."
She answered, "Seven are we;
And two of us at Conway dwell,
And two are gone to sea.

"Two of us in the church-yard lie,
My sister and my brother;
And, in the church-yard cottage, I
Dwell near them with my mother."

"You say that two at Conway dwell,
And two are gone to sea,
Yet ye are seven! I pray you tell,
Sweet Maid, how this may be."

Then did the little Maid reply,
"Seven boys and girls are we;
Two of us in the church-yard lie,
Beneath the church-yard tree."

"You run about, my little Maid,
Your limbs they are alive;
If two are in the church-yard laid,
Then ye are only five."

"Their graves are green, they may be seen,"
The little Maid replied.
"Twelve steps or more from my mother's door,
And they are side by side.

"My stockings there I often knit,
My kerchief there I hem;

And there upon the ground I sit,
And sing a song to them.

"And often after sun-set, Sir,
When it is light and fair,
I take my little porringer,
And eat my supper there.

"The first that died was sister Jane;
In bed she moaning lay,
Till God released her of her pain;
And then she went away.

"So in the church-yard she was laid;
And, when the grass was dry,
Together round her grave we played,
My brother John and I.

"And when the ground was white with snow.
And I could run and slide,
My brother John was forced to go,
And he lies by her side."

"How many are you, then," said I,
"If they two are in heaven?"
Quick was the little Maid's reply,
"O Master! we are seven."

"But they are dead; those two are dead!
Their spirits are in heaven!"
'Twas throwing words away; for still
The little Maid would have her will,
And said, "Nay, we are seven!"

Parents and Children of the Past

Lady Jane Grey speaks of her childhood:

One of the greatest benefits that God ever gave me is, that he sent me so sharpe and severe Parentes. . . . For when I am in presence either of father or mother, whether I speke, kepe silence, sit, stand, or go, eate, drinke, be merie or sad, be sewyng, plaiying, dauncyng, or do aniething els, I must do it, as it were, in such weight, mesure and number, even so perfitlie as God made the world, else I am so sharpelie taunted, so cruelie threatened, yea presentlie some tymes with pinches, nippes, and bobbes, and other waies which I will not name for the honor I bear them. . .that I thinke myself in hell.

1537–1554

Margaret Paston to her son, John . . . 1463

I greet you well, and send you God's blessing and mine; letting you wit that I have received a letter from you the which ye delivered to Master Roger at Lynn, whereby I conceive that ye think ye did not well that ye departed hence

95

without my knowledge. Wherefore I let you wit I was right evil paid with you. Your father thought, and thinketh yet, that I was assented to your departing, and that hath caused me to have great heaviness. I hope he will be your good father hereafter, if ye demean you well and do as you owe to do to him; and I charge you upon my blessing that in anything touching your father that should be his worship, profit or avail, that ye do your devoir and diligent labour to the furtherance therein, and ye will have my good will; and that shall cause your father to be better father to you.

It was told me ye sent him a letter to London. What the intent thereof was I wot not, but though he took it but lightly, I would ye should not spare to write to him again as lowly as ye can, beseeching him to be your good father, and send him such tidings as beth in the country there you beth in; and that ye beware of your expense better (than) ye have be before this time, and be your own purse-bearer. I trow ye shall find it most profitable to you.

I would ye should send me word how ye do, and how you have chevished for yourself sin ye departed hence, by some trusty man, and that your father have no knowledge thereof. I durst not let him know of the last letter ye wrote to me, because he was so sore displeased with me at that time. . . .

. . . . As for your harness and gear that ye left here, it is in Daubeney's keeping. It was never removed sin your departing, because that he had not the keys. . . . Your father knoweth not where it is. I sent your grey horse to Ruston to the farrier, and he saith he shall never be naught to road, neither right good to plough nor to cart. He saith he was splayed, and his shoulder rent from the body. I wot not what to do with him.

Your grandam would fain hear some tidings from you. It were well do that ye sent a letter to her how ye do, as hastily

as ye may. And God have you in his keeping, and make you
a good man, and give you grace to do as well as I would ye
should do. Written at Caister the Tuesday next before St
Edmund the King.

Your mother,

M.Paston.

From *The Paston Letters*, edited by NORMAN DAVIS (1963)

Sir Thomas More to his daughter, Margaret . . . 1535

Sir Thomas More, who was Lord Chancellor to Henry VIII, was a great family man. He educated his daughters, as well as his sons, which was an advanced thing to do. There is a great and famous painting by Holbein of the entire More family gathered together. This letter was written on the eve of Sir Thomas's execution for treason—he could not bring himself to accept the King as Supreme Head of the Church in England. Since all his possessions had been removed from him, the letter was written with a piece of charcoal from the fire; and if there were an address at the top it would be: The Tower of London.

Our Lord bless you, good daughter, and your good husband,
and your little boy, and all yours, and all my children, and
all my god-children, and all our friends. Recommend me
when you may, to my good daughter Cicely, whom I be-
seech our Lord to comfort. And I send her my blessing, and
to all her children, and pray her to pray for me. I send her
an handkerchief: and God comfort my good son, her husband. My good daughter Daunce has the picture in parch-
ment, that you delivered me from my Lady Coniers, her
name is on the back side. Show her that I heartily pray her
that you may send it in my name to her again, for a token
from me to pray for me. I like especial well Dorothy Coly;
I pray you be good unto her. I wonder whether this be she
that you wrote me of. If not yet, I pray you be good to the
other as you may in her affliction, and to my good daughter,
Joan Alyn too. Give her, I pray you, some kind answer, for

she sued hither to me this day to pray you be good to her. I cumber you, good Margaret, much, but I would be sorry if it should be any longer than tomorrow. For it is Saint Thomas' Even, and the Utas of Saint Peter; and therefore tomorrow long I to go to God: it were a day very meet and convenient to me. I never liked your manner toward me better, than when you kissed me last; for I love when daughterly love and dear charity hath no leisure to look to worldly courtesy. Farewell, my dear child, and pray for me, and I shall for all your friends, that we may merrily meet in Heaven. I thank you for your great cost. I send now to my good daughter Clement her algorism stone (*a calculating device*), and I send her and my god-son and all hers God's blessing and mine. I pray you at time convenient recommend me to my good son, John More. I liked well his natural fashion. Our Lord bless him and his good wife, my loving daughter, to whom I pray him to be good as he hath great cause: and that if the land of mine come to his hand, he break not my will concerning his sister Daunce. And our Lord bless Thomas and Austen and all that they shall have.

From *The Life of Sir Thomas More, Knight*, by William Roper (1557)

Sir Henry Sidney to his son Philip, at school . . . 1565

Son Philip,

I have received two letters from you, one written in Latin, the other in French: which I take in good part and will you to exercise that practice of learning often; for that will stand you in most stead in that profession of life that you are born to live in. And now, since this is my first letter that ever I did write to you, I will not that it be all empty of some advices which my natural care of you provoketh me to wish you to follow, as documents to you in this your tender age.

Let your first action be the lifting up of your mind to Almighty God, by hearty prayer; and feelingly digest the words you speak in prayer, with continual meditation and thinking of Him to Whom you pray, and of the matter for which you pray. And use this as an ordinary act, and at an ordinary hour; whereby the time itself shall put you in remembrance to do that you are accustomed to do at that time.

Apply your study to such hours as your discreet master doth assign you, earnestly; and the time I know he will so limit as shall be both sufficient for your learning and safe for your health. And mark the sense and matter of that you do read, as well as the words; so shall you both enrich your tongue with words and your wit with matter, and judgment shall grow as years grow in you.

Be humble and obedient to your masters, for, unless you frame yourself to obey others—yea, and feel in yourself what obedience is, you shall never be able to teach others how to obey you.

Be courteous of gesture and affable to all men, with dignity of reverence, according to the dignity of the person. There is nothing that winneth so much with so little cost.

Use moderate diet, so as, after your meal, you may find your wit fresher and not duller, and your body more lively and not more heavy. Seldom drink wine; and yet sometimes do; lest, being enforced to drink upon the sudden, you should find yourself enflamed. Use exercise of body, yet such as is without peril to your bones or joints: it will increase your force and enlarge your breath. Delight to be cleanly, as well in all parts of your body as in your garments; it shall make you grateful in each company—and otherwise loathsome.

Give yourself to be merry; for you degenerate from your father if you find not yourself most able in wit and body to do anything when you are most merry. But let your mirth be ever void of all scurrility and biting words to any man; for a wound given by a word is oftentimes harder to be cured than that which is given by the sword.

Be you rather a hearer and bearer away of other men's talk than a beginner and procurer of speech: otherwise you shall be accounted to delight to hear yourself speak. If you hear a wise sentence or an apt phrase, commit it to your memory with respect of the circumstance when you shall speak it. Let never oath be heard to come out of your mouth, nor word of ribaldry: so shall custom make to yourself a law against it in yourself. Be modest in each assembly, and rather be rebuked of light fellows for maiden-like shamefastness than of your sad friends for pert boldness. Think upon every word that you will speak before you utter it, and remember how nature hath ramparted up, as it were, the tongue with teeth, lips—yea, and hair without the lips, and all betokening reins and bridles for the loose use of that member.

Above all things, tell no untruth; no, not in trifles. The custom of it is naughty. And let it not satisfy you that for a time the hearers take it for a truth; for after it will be known as it is, to your shame. For there cannot be a greater reproach to a gentleman than to be accounted a liar.

Study and endeavour yourself to be virtuously occupied. So shall you make such a habit of well-doing in you as you shall not know how to do evil, though you would. Remember, my son, the noble blood you are descended of by your mother's side; and think that only by virtuous life and good action you may be an ornament to that illustrious family. . . .

Well, my little Philip, this is enough for me, and too much, I fear, for you. . . .

. . . Farewell! Your mother and I send you our blessings, and Almighty God grant you His, nourish you with His fear, govern you with His grace, and make you a good servant to your prince and country!

Your loving father, so long as you live in the fear of God,

H. Sidney

Lord Chesterfield to his son, being educated abroad . . . 1748

Dear Boy,

 . . . From your own observation, reflect what a disagreeable impression an awkard address, a slovenly figure, an ungraceful manner of speaking whether stuttering, muttering, monotony, or drawling, an unattentive behaviour, etc., make upon you at first sight, in a stranger, and how they prejudice you against him, though, for aught you know, he may have great intrinsic sense and merit. . . . A pretty person, genteel motions, a proper degree of dress, an harmonious voice, something open and cheerful in the countenance, but without laughing; a distinct and properly varied manner of speaking: all these things, and many others, are necessary ingredients in the composition of the pleasing *je ne sçais quoi*, which everybody feels, though 'nobody can describe. Observe carefully, then, what displeases or pleases you in others, and be persuaded that, in general, the same thing will please or displease them in you.

Having mentioned laughing, I must particularly warn you against it; and I could heartily wish that you may often be seen to smile, but never heard to laugh while you live. Frequent and loud laughter is the characteristic of folly and ill manners: it is the manner in which the mob express their silly joy at silly things; and they call it being merry. In my mind there is nothing so illiberal, and so ill-bred, as audible laughter. True wit, or sense, never yet made anybody laugh; they are above it: they please the mind, and give a cheerfulness to the countenance. But it is low buffoonery or silly accidents that always excite laughter; and that is what people of sense and breeding should show themselves above. A man's going to sit down, in the supposition that he had a chair behind him, and falling down upon his breech for want of

one, sets a whole company a-laughing, when all the wit in
the world would not do it; a plain proof, in my mind, how
low and unbecoming a thing laughter is. Not to mention the
disagreeable noise it makes, and the shocking distortion of the
face that it occasions. Laughter is easily restrained by a very
little reflection; but, as it is generally connected with the idea
of gaiety, people do not enough attend to its absurdity. I am
neither a melancholy, nor a cynical disposition; and am as
willing, and as apt, to be pleased as anybody; but I am sure
that, since I have had the use of my reason, nobody has ever
heard me laugh. . . .

From *Letters to His Son*, by Lord Chesterfield (1748)

The Easter Egg

ALISON UTTLEY

*A book about growing up in a countryside very different from today's. Susan
walks four miles to school, and four miles back. The farmhouse is bitterly cold
in winter and there are not many excitements save those to be found in small
events and the changing seasons. In this chapter, Susan makes an excitement of
her own, though she does so by accident.* Margaret *is Susan's mother;* Tom *is
her father;* Roger *is the dog;* Fanny *and* Duchess *are farm animals.*

One morning Susan looked out of her window and saw that
spring had really come. She could smell it and she put her
head far out, until she could touch the budding elm twigs.
She pressed her hands on the rough stone of the window-sill
to keep herself from falling as she took in deep draughts of
the wine-filled air.

It was the elder; the sap was rushing up the pithy stems,
the young leaves had pierced the buds, and now stuck out
like green ears listening to the sounds of spring. The rich
heady smell from the pale speckled branches came in waves,
borne by soft winds, mixed with the pungent odour of young
nettles and dock.

She wrinkled her nose with pleasure and a rabbit with her
little one directly below the window, on the steep slope,

wrinkled her nose, too, as she sat up among the nettles and
borage.

Miss Susanna Dickory, Susan's godmother, had stayed at
the farm a fortnight, and now Susan felt lost without her. It
had been a time of delight to meet lavender in pockets of air
on the stairs. Such delicious smells hovered about the house,
such rustlings of silken skirts, and yap-yaps of the little be-
ribboned, long-haired dog, Twinkle, as unlike Roger as a toy
boat is unlike a man-o'-war.

"Twinkle, Twinkle, Twinkle," she called in her high silvery
voice, which made Dan laugh up his sleeve. It was for all the
world like the harness bells, he told Becky.

She had come to visit her dear friend, Margaret, and to
see her little god-child, Susan, and if she was disappointed in
the child and found her a shy young colt, she said nothing.

She was a frail old lady, delicate-looking and fastidious,
but she walked in the cow-sheds and sat down in the barns
with her silk petticoats trailing in the dust, so that Joshua ran
for the besom to sweep before her, and he actually took off
his coat for her to step upon, like Sir Walter Raleigh, but
Miss Dickory wouldn't.

Every day the Garlands had dinner and tea in the parlour
and every day the Worcester china was used. Becky put on
a clean white cap and apron, and Dan brushed his coat
and changed his collar, and scrubbed all the manure off
his boots before he sat down in the kitchen, lest she should
come in.

She slept in the big four-poster in the parlour bedroom and
wore a lace night-cap, for Susan saw it when Becky took up
her breakfast on a tray. Twinkle slept in a basket lined with
silk at the foot of her bed. It was all most astonishing, like
being in church all the time, and Christmas every day.

But now she had gone and only a few little corners of sweet

smells remained. Susan sighed as she thought of her, and laughed at the rabbit, and then ran downstairs. It was Good Friday and she had a holiday for a week.

Her mother met her in the hall, running excitedly to call her. There was a parcel addressed to Mr. Mrs., and Miss Garland. Susan had never been called Miss before, except by the old man at the village who said, "You're late, Missie," when she ran past his cottage on the way to school.

With trembling fingers Susan and Margaret untied the knots, for never, never had anyone at Windystone been so wasteful as to cut a piece of string.

Inside was a flower-embroidered table-cloth for Margaret, a book of the Christian Saints and Martyrs of the Church for Tom, which he took with wondering eyes, and a box containing six Easter eggs.

There were three chocolate eggs, covered with silver paper, a wooden egg painted with pictures round the edge, a red egg with a snake inside, and a beautiful pale blue velvet egg lined with golden starry paper. It was a dream. Never before had Susan seen anything so lovely. Only once had she ever seen an Easter egg (for such luxuries were not to be found in the shops at Broomy Vale), and then it had been associated with her disgrace.

Last Easter Mrs. Garland had called at the vicarage with her missionary box and taken Susan with her. Mrs. Stone had asked Margaret to make some shirts for the heathen, and whilst they had gone in the sewing-room to look at the pattern, Susan, who had been sitting silent and shy on the edge of her chair, was left alone.

The room chattered to her; she sprang up, wide-awake, and stared around. She had learnt quite a lot about the habits of the family from the table and chairs, when her eye unfortunately spied a fat chocolate egg, a bloated enormous

egg, on a desk before the window. Round its stomach was
tied a blue ribbon, like a sash.

Susan gazed in astonishment. What was it for? She put out
a finger and stroked its glossy surface. Then she gave it a tiny
press of encouragement, and, oh! her finger went through and
left a little hole. The egg must have been soft with the sunshine. But who would have thought it was hollow, a sham?

She ran and sat down again, deliberating whether to say
something at once or to wait till she was alone with her
mother. Mrs. Stone returned with Margaret saying, "Yes,
Mrs. Stone, of course I won't forget the gussets. The heathen
jump about a good deal, they will need plenty of room." But
before Susan could speak, a long-haired, beaky-nosed girl ran
into the room, stared at Susan and went straight to the Easter
egg.

"Who's been touching my Easter egg?" she cried, just like
the three bears.

They all looked at Susan and with deep blushes she
whispered, "I did."

They all talked at once, Margaret was full of apologies and
shame, Mrs. Stone said it didn't matter, but of course you
could see it did, and the bear rumbled and growled.

When she got home Susan had to kneel down at once and
say a prayer for forgiveness, although it was the middle of the
morning. "You know, Susan, it's very wrong to touch what
isn't yours."

But this perfect blue egg! There was never one like it. She
put it in her little drawer in the table where her treasures
were kept, the book of pressed flowers, the book of texts in
the shape of a bunch of violets, the velvet Christmas card
with the silk fringe, and the card that came this Christmas.

Tenderly she touched them all. In the egg she placed her
ring with the red stone, and a drop of quicksilver which had

come from the barometer. She closed the drawer and went off to tell anyone who would listen, the trees, Dan, the clock, Roger, Duchess, or Fanny.

But what a tale to tell the girls at school! She wouldn't take it there or it might get hurt, a rough boy might snatch it from her, or the teacher might see her with it and put it in her desk.

"Mother, may I ask someone to tea to see my egg?" she asked, fearing in her heart that no one would come so far.

"Yes, my dear," and Margaret smiled at her enthusiasm, "ask whoever you like."

She hurried through the woods and along the lanes to school, saying to herself, "Do you know what I had at Easter? No. Guess what I had at Easter. No. My godmother, who is a real lady, sent me such a lovely Easter present. It was a box of eggs, and one was made of sky-blue velvet and lined with golden stars."

She was late and had to run, and when she passed the little cottage with the brass door-knocker and a canary in the window, the nice old man with a beard said, "You are going to be late this morning, Missie," as he looked at his turnip watch. It was very kind of him, and Susan thanked him politely before she took to her heels.

She toiled up the hill, a stitch in her side, and her face wet with perspiration, past the cottages with babies at the open doors and cats by the fire, past the silent gabled house where two old ladies lived, and the old cottage where the witch pottered about, and the lovely farm where she sometimes went to tea with her mother, and sat very still listening to the ancient man who lived there.

The bell stopped ringing and she was late. She would be caned, she had no excuse. She heard the Lord's Prayer and the hymn as she took off her hat and cape, and hung them on the hook. She listened to the high voices and watched the door handle, waiting to slip in at the sound of Amen. Her little red tongue glided over the palm of her hand, to prepare for the inevitable. There was a shuffle of feet and she turned the knob. All eyes switched her way as she walked up to the desk.

"Any excuse, Susan Garland?"

She dumbly held out her hand. Down came the cane three times on the soft flesh. Biting her lip and keeping back her tears she walked to her place, and bound her handkerchief round the hot stinging palm. Yes, there were three marks, three red stripes across it.

Curious eyes watched her to see if she would cry, and she smiled round and whispered, "It didn't hurt a bit", but her hand throbbed under her pinafore, and the fingers curled protectingly round it as if they were sorry. It was an honour to be caned and to bear the strokes unflinchingly. Susan showed her marks to the girls round her, and then whispered, "I've got a blue velvet egg. Tell you about it at playtime."

At break the children walked orderly to the door and then flung themselves out into the playground, to jump and "twizzle", hop and skip, to dig in their gardens, or play hide-and-seek.

Susan had a circle of girls round her looking at the weals and listening to the tale of the egg. They strolled under the chestnut trees with their arms round each other.

"It's blue velvet, sky-blue, and inside it is lined with paper covered with gold stars. It's the most beautiful egg I ever saw." The girls opened their eyes and shook their curls in amazement.

"Bring it to school for us to see," said Anne Frost, her friend.

"I daren't, Mother wouldn't let me, but you can come to tea and see it."

"Can I?" asked one. "Can I?" asked another.

Susan felt like a queen and invited them all. Big girls came to her, and she invited them. The rumour spread that Susan Garland was having a lot of girls to tea. Tiny little girls ran up and she said they might come too. She didn't know where to draw the line, and in the end the whole school of girls invited themselves.

They ran home to Dangle and Raddle at dinner-time to say that Susan Garland was having a party, and they were brushed and washed and put into clean pinafores and frocks, with blue necklaces and Sunday hair-ribbons.

Susan sat on a low stone wall eating her sandwiches, excited and happy. She was sure they would all be welcome and she looked forward to the company in the Dark Wood.

After school she started off with a crowd of fifty girls, holding each other's hands, arms entwined round Susan's waist, all pressed up close to her. They filled the narrow road like a migration, or the Israelites leaving the bondage of Egypt.

Mothers came to their doors to see them pass, and waved their hands to their little daughters. "Those Garlands must have plenty of money," said they.

Susan was filled with pride to show her beautiful home, the fields and buildings, the haystacks, the bull, and her kind mother and father, and Becky and Joshua who would receive them.

They went noisily through the wood, chattering and gay, astonished at the long journey and the darkness of the trees, clinging to one another on the little path lest an adder or fox should come out, giggling and pushing each other into the leaves. The squirrels looked down in wonder, and all ghostly things fled.

Margaret happened to stand on the bank that day to watch for Susan's appearance at the end of the wood; she always felt slightly anxious if the child were late.

She could scarcely believe her eyes. There was Susan in her grey cape and the new scarlet tam-o'-shanter, but with her came a swarm of children. She had forgotten all about the vague invitation.

Was the child bringing the whole school home?

She ran back to the house and called Becky and Joshua. They stood dumbfounded, looking across the fields.

"We shall have to give them all something to eat, coming all that way," she groaned.

"It will be like feeding the five thousand in the Bible," exclaimed Becky, and Joshua stood gaping. He had never known such a thing. What had come over the little maid to ask such a rabble?

They went to the kitchen and dairy to take stock. There was Becky's new batch of bread, the great earthenware crock full to the brim, standing on the larder floor. There was a dish of butter ready for the shops, and baskets of eggs counted out, eighteen a shilling. There was a tin of brandy snaps, to last for months, some enormous jam pasties, besides three plum cakes.

They set to work, cutting and spreading on the big table, filling bread and butter plates with thick slices.

Joshua filled the copper kettles and put them on the fire, and counted out four dozen eggs, which he put on to boil. "We can boil more when we've counted the lasses."

Roger nearly went crazy when he saw the tribe come straggling and tired up the path to the front of the house. Susan left them resting on the wall and went in to her mother.

"I've brought some girls to tea, Mother," she said, opening her eyes at the preparations.

"Oh, indeed," said Mrs. Garland. "How many have you brought?"

"A lot," answered Susan. "Where's my egg, they want to see it?"

"Susan Garland," said Margaret severely, taking her by the shoulders, "whatever do you mean by bringing all those girls home with you? Don't talk about that egg. Don't you see that they must all be fed? We can't let them come all this way without a good tea. You mustn't think of the egg, you will have to work."

Susan looked aghast, she realized what she had done and
began to cry.

"Never mind, dry your eyes at once and smile. I don't
know what your father will say, but we will try to get them
fed before he comes."

Margaret began to enjoy herself, she was a born hostess and
here was a chance to exercise her hospitality.

She went out to the children and invited them to have a wash at the back door, where she had put a pancheon of hot water and towels. Then they were to sit orderly on the low walls, along the front of the house, and wait for tea which would come out in a few minutes. She chose four girls to help to carry the things, and then she returned, leaving smiles and anticipation.

The fifty trooped round the house and washed their hands and faces, with laughter and glee. They peeped at the troughs, and admired the pig-cotes, but Susan shepherded them back to the walls where they sat in their white pinafores like swallows ready for flight.

Becky and Joshua carried out the great copper tea-urn, which was used at farm suppers and sometimes lent for church parties. Margaret collected every cup and mug, basin and bowl in the house, from the capacious kitchen cupboards and tall-boy, the parlour cupboards, the shelves, the dressers, from corner cupboards upstairs, from china cabinet stand, and what-not, from brackets and pedestals.

There were Jubilee mugs, and gold lustre mugs, an old china mug with "Susan Garland, 1840", on it, and several with "A present for a Good Girl". There were mugs with views and mugs with wreaths of pink and blue flowers, with mottoes and proverbs, with old men in high hats and women in wide skirts. There were tin mugs which belonged to the Irishmen, and Sheffield plated mugs from the mantelpiece, pewter and earthenware. There were delicate cups of lovely china, decorated with flowers and birds, blue Wedgwood, and some Spode breakfast cups, besides little basins and fluted bowls.

Margaret gave out the cups and mugs herself, choosing clean, careful-looking girls for her best china. The social position of each girl could be detected at once from the kind of cup she had, which was unlike Margaret's usual procedure, but this was an exceptional occasion. If only they had been round a table she would have trusted them, but now she had to use her judgement.

Becky poured out the tea, and Susan took it to each girl, with new milk and brown sugar. Old Joshua, wearing an apron, walked along the rows with a clothes-basket of bread and butter and a basket of eggs. As soon as he got to the end he began again.

Margaret took over the tea, and sent Becky to cut more and more. Susan's legs ached and an immense hunger seized her, she had eaten nothing but sandwiches since her breakfast at half past seven. But there was no time, the girls clamoured for more, and she ran backwards and forwards with her four helpers, who had their own tea in between.

A clothes-basket was filled with cut-up pieces of cake, pastry, slabs of the men's cake, apple pastry, and currant slices. Then the box of ginger-snaps was taken round, and some girls actually refused. The end was approaching, but still Joshua walked up and down the line with food.

Dan came out from the cow-houses with the milk, and Tom followed. Nobody had been in the smaller cow-houses. What was Joshua doing in an apron, and Becky too when she should be milking?

He stared at the rows of chattering children and walked in the house. Margaret ran in to explain.

"Don't be cross with her," she said.

He said nothing till Susan came in for more cake.

Then he stood up and looked at her, and Susan quailed.

"Dang my buttons, Susan Garland, if you are not the most silly soft lass I ever knew! Are you clean daft crazy to bring all that crowd of cackling childer here?"

Then he stamped out to the byres and Susan walked back

with her slices of cake, thankful she had not been sent to bed.

At last the feast was finished and Becky and Margaret washed up the cups and mugs, and collected the egg-shells, whilst Joshua went milking and Susan ran for a ball to give them a game in the field before they went home. They ran races and played hide-and-seek, and lerky, they played ticky-ticky-touch-stone round the great menhir, and swarmed over its surface.

At the end of an hour Margaret rang a bell and they came racing to her. "Put on your coats now, my dears, and go home, your mothers will expect you, and you have a long walk before you."

So they said goodbye, and ran off singing and happy, down the hill. Two little girls had come shyly up to Susan with a parcel before they went.

"Mother said if it was your birthday we were to give you this," and they held out a ball like a pineapple. But Susan had to confess it wasn't her birthday and they took it home.

She went indoors and sat down, tired and famished, at the table. "And, Mother, I never showed them my sky-blue egg after all! But they did enjoy themselves."

From *The Country Child* (1931)

The Kitchen

LAURIE LEE

Our house, and our life in it, is something of which I still constantly dream, helplessly bidden, night after night, to return to its tranquillity and nightmares: to the heavy shadows of its stone-walled rooms creviced between bank and yew trees, to its boarded ceilings and gaping mattresses, its blood-shot geranium windows, its smells of damp pepper and mushroom growths, its chaos, and rule of women.

We boys never knew any male authority. My father left us when I was three, and apart from some rare and fugitive visits he did not live with us again. He was a knowing, brisk, elusive man, the son and the grandson of sailors, but having himself no stomach for the sea he had determined to make good on land. In his miniature way he succeeded in this. He became, while still in his middle teens, a grocer's assistant, a local church organist, an expert photographer and a dandy. Certain portraits he took of himself at that time show a handsome though threadbare lad, tall and slender and much addicted to gloves, high-collars and courtly poses. He was clearly a cut above the average, in charm as well as ambition.

By the age of twenty he had married the beautiful daughter of a local merchant, and she bore him eight children—of whom five survived—before dying herself still young. Then he married his housekeeper, who bore him four more, three surviving, of which I was one. At the time of this second marriage he was still a grocer's assistant, and earning nineteen shillings a week. But his dearest wish was to become a Civil Servant, and he studied each night to this end. The First World War gave him the chance he wanted, and though properly distrustful of arms and battle he instantly sacrificed both himself and his family, applied for a post in the Army Pay Corps, went off to Greenwich in a bullet-proof vest and never permanently lived with us again.

He was a natural fixer, my father was, and things worked out pretty smoothly. He survived his clerk-stool war with a War Office pension (for nervous rash, I believe), then entered the Civil Service, as he had planned to do, and settled in London for good. Thus enabling my Mother to raise both his families, which she did out of love and pity, out of unreasoning loyalty and a fixed belief that he would one day return to her. . . .

Meanwhile, we lived where he had left us; a relic of his provincial youth; a sprawling, cumbersome, countrified brood too incongruous to carry with him. He sent us money, and we grew up without him; and I, for one, scarcely missed him. I was perfectly content in this world of women, muddle-headed though it might be, to be bullied and tumbled through the hand-to-mouth days, patched or dressed-up, scolded, admired, swept off my feet in sudden passions of kisses, or dumped forgotten among the unwashed pots.

My three half-sisters shared much of Mother's burden, and were the good fortune of our lives. Generous, indulgent,

warm-blooded and dotty, these girls were not hard to admire.
They seemed wrapped as it were in a perpetual bloom, the
glamour of their grown-up teens, and expressed for us boys
all that women should be in beauty, style and artifice.

For there was no doubt at all about their beauty, or the
naturalness with which they wore it. Marjorie, the eldest, a
blonde Aphrodite, appeared quite unconscious of the rarity
of herself, moving always to measures of oblivious grace and
wearing her beauty like a kind of sleep. She was tall, long-
haired and dreamily gentle, and her voice was low and slow.
I never knew her to lose her temper, or to claim any personal
justice. But I knew her to weep, usually for others, quietly,
with large blue tears. She was a natural mother, and skilled
with her needle, making clothes for us all when needed. With
her constant beauty and balanced nature she was the tranquil
night-light of our fears, a steady flame reassuring always,
whose very shadows seemed thrown for our comfort.

Dorothy, the next one, was a wispy imp, pretty and perilous
as a firework. Compounded equally of curiosity and cheek, a
spark and tinder for boys, her quick dark body seemed writ
with warnings that her admirers did well to observe. "Not to
be held in the hand," it said. "Light the touch-paper, but
retire immediately." She was an active forager who lived on
thrills, provoked adventure and brought home gossip.
Marjorie's were the ears to which most of it came, making
her pause in her sewing, open wide her eyes and shake her
head at each new revelation. "You don't mean it, Doth! He
never! No! . . ." was all I seemed ever to hear.

Dorothy was as agile as a jungle cat, quick-limbed, en-
trancing, noisy. And she protected us boys with fire and
spirit, and brought us treasures from the outside world.
When I think of her now she is a coil of smoke, a giggling
splutter, a reek of cordite. In repose she was also something

else: a fairy-tale girl, blue as a plum, tender and sentimental.

The youngest of the three was cool, quiet Phyllis, a tobacco-haired, fragile girl, who carried her good looks with an air of apology, being the junior and somewhat shadowed. Marjorie and Dorothy shared a natural intimacy, being closer together in age, so Phyllis was the odd one, an unclassified solitary, compelled to her own devices. This she endured with a modest simplicity, quick to admire and slow to complain. Her favourite chore was putting us boys to bed, when she emerged in a strange light of her own, revealing a devout almost old-fashioned watchfulness, and gravely singing us to sleep with hymns.

Sad Phyllis, lit by a summer night, her tangled hair aglow, quietly sitting beside our beds, hands folded, eyes far away, singing and singing of "Happy Eden" alone with her care over us—how often to this did I drop into sleep, feel the warmth of its tide engulf me, steered by her young hoarse hymning voice and tuneless reveries. . . .

These half-sisters I cherished; and apart from them I had two half-brothers also. Reggie, the first-born, lived apart with his grandmother; but young Harold, he lived with us. Harold was handsome, bony and secretive, and he loved our absent father. He stood somewhat apart, laughed down his nose, and was unhappy more often than not. Though younger than the girls, he seemed a generation older, was clever with his hands, but lost.

My own true brothers were Jack and Tony, and we three came at the end of the line. We were of Dad's second marriage, before he flew, and were born within the space of four years. Jack was the eldest, Tony the youngest, and myself the protected centre. Jack was the sharp one, bright as a knife, and was also my close companion. We played together, fought and ratted, built a private structure around us, shared the same bed till I finally left home, and lived off each other's brains. Tony, the baby—strange and beautiful waif—was a brooding, imaginative solitary. Like Phyllis he suffered from being the odd one of three; worse still, he was the odd one of seven. He was always either running to keep up with the rest of us or sitting alone in the mud. His curious, crooked, suffering face had at times the radiance of a saint, at others the blank watchfulness of an insect. He could walk by himself or keep very still, get lost or appear at wrong moments. He drew like an artist, wouldn't read or write, swallowed beads by the boxful, sang and danced, was quite without fear, had secret friends, and was prey to terrible nightmares. Tony was the one true visionary amongst us, the tiny hermit no one quite understood. . . .

With our Mother, then, we made eight in that cottage and disposed of its three large floors. There was the huge white attic which ran the length of the house, where the girls slept on fat striped mattresses; an ancient, plaster-crumbling room whose sloping ceilings bulged like tent-cloths. The roof was so thin that rain and bats filtered through, and you could hear a bird land on the tiles. Mother and Tony shared a bedroom below; Jack, Harold and I the other. But the house, since its building, had been so patched and parcelled that it was now almost impossible to get to one's room without first passing through someone else's. So each night saw a procession of pallid ghosts, sleepily seeking their beds, till the candle-snuffed darkness laid us out in rows, filed away in our allotted sheets, while snores and whistles shook the old house like a roundabout getting up steam.

But our waking life, and our growing years, were for the most part spent in the kitchen, and until we married, or ran away, it was the common room we shared. Here we lived

and fed in a family fug, not minding the little space, trod on each other like birds in a hole, elbowed our ways without spite, all talking at once or all silent at once, or crying against each other, but never I think feeling overcrowded, being as separate as notes in a scale.

That kitchen, worn by our boots and lives, was scruffy, warm and low, whose fuss of furniture seemed never the same but was shuffled around each day. A black grate crackled with coal and beech-twigs; towels toasted on the guard; the mantel was littered with fine old china, horse brasses and freak potatoes. On the floor were strips of muddy matting, the windows were choked with plants, the walls supported stopped clocks and calendars, and smoky fungus ran over the ceilings. There were also six tables of different sizes, some armchairs gapingly stuffed, boxes, stools and unravelling baskets, books and papers on every chair, a sofa for cats, a harmonium for coats, and a piano for dust and photographs.

These were the shapes of our kitchen landscape, the rocks of our submarine life, each object worn smooth by our constant nuzzling, or encrusted by lively barnacles, relics of birthdays and dead relations, wrecks of furniture long since foundered, all silted deep by mother's newspapers which the years piled round on the floor.

Waking up in the morning I saw squirrels in the yew trees nibbling at the moist red berries. Between the trees and the window hung a cloud of gold air composed of floating seeds and spiders. Farmers called to their cows on the other side of the valley and moorhens piped from the ponds. Brother Jack, as always, was the first to move, while I pulled on my boots in bed. We both stood at last on the bare-wood floor, scratching and saying our prayers. Too stiff and manly to say them out loud, we stood back to back and muttered them, and if an audible plea should slip out by chance, one just burst into song to cover it.

Singing and whistling were useful face-savers, especially when confounded by argument. We used the trick readily, one might say monotonously, and this morning it was Jack who began it.

"What's the name of the king, then?" he said, groping for his trousers.

"Albert."

"No, it's not. It's George."

"That's what I said you, didn't I? George."

"No you never. You don't know. You're feeble."

"Not so feeble as you be, any road."

"You're balmy. You got brains of a bed-bug."

"Da-da-di-da-da."

"I said you're brainless. You can't even count."

"Turrelee-turrelie. . . . Didn't hear you."

"Yes you did then, blockhead. Fat and lazy. Big faa—"

"Dum-di-dah! . . . Can't hear . . . Hey nonnie! . . ."

Well, that was all right; honours even, as usual. We broke the sleep from our eyes and dressed quickly.

Walking downstairs there was a smell of floorboards, of rags, sour lemons, old spices. The smoky kitchen was in its morning muddle, from which breakfast would presently emerge. Mother stirred the porridge in a soot-black pot. Tony was carving bread with a ruler, the girls in their mackintoshes were laying the table, and the cats were eating the butter. I cleaned some boots and pumped up some fresh water; Jack went for a jug of skimmed milk.

"I'm all behind," Mother said to the fire. "This wretched coal's all slack."

She snatched up an oil-can and threw it all on the fire. A

belch of flame roared up the chimney. Mother gave a loud scream, as she always did, and went on stirring the porridge.

"If I had a proper stove," she said. "It's a trial getting you off each day."

I sprinkled some sugar on a slice of bread and bolted it down while I could. How different again looked the kitchen this morning, swirling with smoke and sunlight. Some cut-glass vases threw jagged rainbows across the piano's field of dust, while Father in his pince-nez up on the wall looked down like a scandalized god.

At last the porridge was dabbed on our plates from a thick and steaming spoon. I covered the smoky lumps with treacle and began to eat from the sides to the middle. The girls round the table chewed moonishly, wrapped in their morning stupor. Still sick with sleep, their mouths moved slow, hung slack while their spoon came up; then they paused for a moment, spoon to lip, collected their wits, and ate. Their vacant eyes stared straight before them, glazed at the sight of the day. Pink and glowing from their dreamy beds, from who knows what arms of heroes, they seemed like mute spirits hauled back to the earth after paradise feasts of love.

"Golly!" cried Doth. "Have you seen the time?"

They began to jump to their feet.

"Goodness, it's late."

"I got to be off."

"Me too."

"Lord, where's my things?"

"Well, ta-ta Ma; ta boys—be good."

"Anything you want up from the Stores . . .?"

They hitched up their stockings, patted their hats and went running up the bank. This was the hour when walkers and bicyclists flowed down the long hills to Stroud, when the hooters called through the morning dews and factories puffed out their plumes. From each crooked corner of Stroud's five valleys girls were running to shops and looms, with sleep in their eyes, and eggy cheeks, and in their ears night voices fading. Marjorie was off to her Milliner's Store, Phyllis to her Boots-and-Shoes, Dorothy to her job as junior clerk in a decayed cloth-mill by a stream. As for Harold, he'd started work already, his day began at six, when he'd leave the house with an angry shout for the lathe-work he really loved.

But what should we boys do, now they had all gone? If it was school-time, we pushed off next. If not, we dodged up the bank to play, ran snail races along the walls, or dug in the garden and found potatoes and cooked them in tins on the rubbish heap. We were always hungry, always calling for food, always seeking it in cupboards and hedges. But holiday mornings were a time of risk, there might be housework or errands to do. Mother would be ironing, or tidying-up, or reading books on the floor. So if we hung round the yard we kept our ears cocked; if she caught us, the game was up.

"Ah, there you are, son. I'm needing some salt. Pop to Vick's for a lump, there's a dear."

Or: "See if Granny Trill's got a screw of tea—only ask her nicely, mind."

Or: "Run up to Miss Turk and try and borrow half-a-crown; I didn't know I'd got so low."

"Ask our Jack, our mother! I borrowed the bacon. It's blummin'-well his turn now."

But Jack had slid off like an eel through the grass, making his sly get-away as usual. He was jumpy, shifty and quick-off-the-mark, an electric flex of nerves, skinny compared with the rest of us, or what farmers might call a "poor doer". If they had, in fact, they would have been quite wrong, for Jack did himself very well. He had developed a mealtime strategy which ensured that he ate for two. Speed and guile

were the keys to his success, and we hungry ones called him
The Slider.

Jack ate against time, that was really his secret; and in our
house you had to do it. Imagine us all sitting down to dinner;
eight round a pot of stew. It was lentil-stew usually, a heavy
brown mash made apparently of plastic studs. Though it
smelt of hot stables, we were used to it, and it was filling
enough—could you get it. But the size of our family out-
stripped the size of the pot, so there was never quite enough
to go round.

When it came to serving, Mother had no method, not even
the law of chance—a dab on each plate in any old order and
then every man for himself. No grace, no warning, no
starting-gun; but the first to finish what he'd had on his
plate could claim what was left in the pot. Mother's swooping
spoon was breathlessly watched—let the lentils fall where
they may. But starveling Jack had worked it all out, he
followed the spoon with his plate. Absentmindedly Mother
would give him first dollop, and very often a second, and as
soon as he got it he swallowed it whole, not using his teeth
at all. "More please, I've finished"—the bare plate proved it,
so he got the pot-scrapings too. Many's the race I've lost to
him thus, being just that second slower. But it left me marked
with an ugly scar, a twisted, food-crazed nature, so that still
I am calling for whole rice puddings and big pots of stew in
the night.

The day was over and we had used it, running errands or
prowling the fields. When evening came we returned to the
kitchen, back to its smoky comfort, in from the rapidly cooling
air to its wrappings of warmth and cooking. We boys came
first, scuffling down the bank, singly, like homing crows.
Long tongues of shadows licked the curves of the fields and

the trees turned plump and still. I had been off to Painswick to pay the rates, running fast through the long wet grass, and now I was back, panting hard, the job finished, with hay seeds stuck to my legs. A plate of blue smoke hung above our chimney, flat in the motionless air, and every stone in the path as I ran down home shook my bones with arriving joy.

We chopped wood for the night and carried it in; dry beech sticks as brittle as candy. The baker came down with a basket of bread slung carelessly over his shoulder. Eight quartern loaves, cottage-size, black-crusted, were handed in at the door. A few crisp flakes of pungent crust still clung to his empty basket, so we scooped them up on our spit-wet fingers and laid them upon our tongues. The twilight gathered, the baker shouted good-night, and whistled his way up the bank. Up in the road his black horse waited, the cart lamps smoking red.

Indoors, our mother was cooking pancakes, her face aglow from the fire. There was a smell of sharp lemon and salty batter, and a burning hiss of oil. The kitchen was dark and convulsive with shadows, no lights had yet been lit. Flames leapt, subsided, corners woke and died, fires burned in a thousand brasses.

"Poke round for the matches, dear boy," said Mother. "Damn me if I know where they got to."

We lit the candles and set them about, each in its proper order: two on the mantelpiece, one on the piano, and one on a plate in the window. Each candle suspended a ball of light, a luminous fragile glow, which swelled and contracted to the spluttering wick or leaned to the moving air. Their flames pushed weakly against the red of the fire, too tenuous to make much headway, revealing our faces more by casts of darkness than by any clear light they threw.

Next we filled and lit the tall iron lamp and placed it on

the table. When the wick had warmed and was drawing properly, we turned it up full strength. The flame in the funnel then sprang alive and rose like a pointed flower, began to sing and shudder and grow more radiant, throwing pools of light on the ceiling. Even so, the kitchen remained mostly in shadow, its walls a voluptuous gloom.

The time had come for my violin practice. I began twanging the strings with relish. Mother was still frying and rolling up pancakes; my brothers lowered their heads and sighed. I propped my music on the mantelpiece and sliced through a Russian Dance while sweet smells of resin mixed with lemon and fat as the dust flew in clouds from my bow. Now and then I got a note just right, and then Mother would throw me a glance. A glance of piercing, anxious encouragement as she side-stepped my swinging arm. Plump in her slippers, one hand to her cheek, her pan beating time in the other, her hair falling down about her ears, mouth working to help out the tune—old and tired though she was, her eyes were a girl's, and it was for looks such as these that I played.

"Splendid!" she cried. "Top-hole! Clap-clap! Now give us another, me lad."

So I slashed away at "William Tell", and when I did that, plates jumped; and Mother skipped gaily around the hearth-rug, and even Tony rocked a bit in his chair.

Meanwhile Jack had cleared some boots from the table and started his inscrutable homework. Tony, in his corner, began to talk to the cat and play with some fragments of cloth. So with the curtains drawn close and the pancakes coming, we settled down to the evening. When the kettle boiled and the toast was made, we gathered and had our tea. We grabbed and dodged and passed and snatched, and packed our mouths like pelicans.

Mother ate always standing up, tearing crusts off the loaf

with her fingers, a hand-to-mouth feeding that expressed her vigilance, like that of a wireless-operator at sea. For most of Mother's attention was fixed on the grate, whose fire must never go out. When it threatened to do so she became seized with hysteria, wailing and wringing her hands, pouring on oil and chopping up chairs in a frenzy to keep it alive. In fact it seldom went out completely, though it was very often ill. But Mother nursed it with skill, banking it up every night and blowing hard on the bars every morning. The state of our fire became as important to us as it must have been to a primitive tribe. When it sulked and sank we were filled with dismay; when it blazed all was well with the world; but if— God save us—it went out altogether, then we were clutched by primeval chills. Then it seemed that the very sun had died, that winter had come for ever, that the wolves of the wilderness were gathering near, and that there was no more hope to look for. . . .

But tonight the firelight snapped and crackled, and Mother was in full control. She ruled the range and all its equipment with a tireless, nervous touch. Eating with one hand, she threw on wood with the other, raked the ashes and heated the oven, put on a kettle, stirred the pot, and spread out some more shirts on the guard. As soon as we boys had finished our tea, we pushed all the crockery aside, piled it up roughly at the far end of the table, and settled down under the lamp. Its light was warm and live around us, a kind of puddle of fire of its own. I set up my book and began to draw. Jack worked at his notes and figures. Tony was playing with some cotton reels, pushing them slowly round the table.

All was silent except for Tony's voice, softly muttering his cotton-reel story.

". . . So they come out of this big hole see, and the big chap said Fie he said we'll kill 'em see, and the pirates was waiting up 'ere, and they had this gurt cannon and they went bang fire and the big chap fell down wheeee! and rolled back in the 'ole and I said we got 'em and I run up the 'ill and this boat see was comin' and I jumped on board wooosh cruump and I said now I'm captain see and they said fie and I took me 'achet 'ack 'ack and they all fell plop in the sea wallop and I sailed the boat round 'ere and round 'ere and up 'ere and round 'ere and down 'ere and up 'ere and round 'ere and down 'ere . . . ."

Now the girls arrived home in their belted mackintoshes, flushed from their walk through the dark, and we looked up from our games and said: "Got anything for us?" and Dorothy gave us some liquorice. Then they all had their supper at one end of the table while we boys carried on at the other. When supper was over and cleared away, the kitchen fitted us all. We drew together round the evening lamp, the vast and easy time. . . . Marjorie began to trim a new hat, Dorothy to write a love-letter, Phyllis sat down with some forks and spoons, blew ah! and sleepily rubbed them. Harold, home late, cleaned his bike in a corner. Mother was cutting up newspapers.

We talked in spurts, in lowered voices, scarcely noticing if anyone answered.

"I turned a shaft to a thou' today," said Harold.

"A what?"

"He said a 'thou'."

Chairs creaked awhile as we thought about it. . . .

"Charlie Revell's got a brand new suit. He had it made to fit. . . ."

"He half fancies himself."

"Charlie Revell! . . ."

Pause.

"Look, Doth, I got these bits for sixpence. I'm going to stitch 'em all round the top here."

"Mmmmm. Well. Tccch-tcch. S'all right . . . "

"Dr Green came up to the shop this morning. Wearing corduroy bloomers. Laugh! . . ."

"Look, Ma, look! I've drawn a church on fire. Look, Marge, Doth! Hey, look! . . ."

"If x equals x, then y equals z—shut up!—if x is y . . ."

"O Madeline, if you'll be mine, I'll take you o'er the sea, di-dah . . ."

"Look what I've cut for my scrapbook, girls—a Beefeater —isn't he killing?"

"Charlie Revell cheeked his dad today. He called him a dafty. He . . ."

". . . You know that boy from the Dairy, Marge—the one they call Barnacle Boots? Well, he asked me to go to Spot's with him. I told him to run off home."

"No! You never!"

"I certainly did. I said I don't go to no pictures with butter-wallopers. You should have seen his face . . . "

"Harry Lazbury smells of chicken-gah. I had to move me desk."

"Just hark who's talking. Dainty Dick."

"I'll never be ready by Sunday . . . "

"I've found a lovely snip for my animal page—an old seal —look girls, the expression! . . . "

"So I went round 'ere, and down round 'ere, and he said fie so I went 'ack, 'ack . . ."

"What couldn't I do to a nice cream slice . . . "

"Charlie Revell's had 'is ears syringed . . . "

"D'you remember, Doth, when we went to Spots, and they said Children in Arms Not Allowed, and we walked little Tone right up the steps and he wasn't even two. . . . "

Marge gave her silky, remembering laugh and looked fondly across at Tony. The fire burned clear with a bottle-green light. Their voices grew low and furry. A farm-dog barked across the valley, fixing the time and distance exactly. Warned by the dog and some hooting owls, I could sense the night valley emptying, stretching in mists of stars and water, growing slowly more secret and late.

The kitchen, warm and murmuring now, vibrated with rosy darkness. My pencil began to wander on the page, my eyes to cloud and clear. I thought I'd stretch myself out on the sofa—for a while, for a short while only. The girls' muted chatter went on and on; I struggled to catch the drift. "Sh! ... Not now. ... When the boys are in bed. ... You'll die when you hear. ... Not now. ..."

The boards on the ceiling were melting like water. Words broke and went floating away. Chords of smooth music surged up in my head, thick tides of warmth overwhelmed me, I was drowning in languors of feathered seas, spiralling cosily down. ...

Once in a while I was gently roused to a sound amplified by sleep; to the fall of a coal, the sneeze of the cat, or a muted exclamation. "She couldn't have done such a thing. ... She did. ... Done what? ... What thing? ... Tell, tell me. ..." But helpless I glided back to sleep, deep in the creviced seas, the blind waters stilled me, weighed me down, the girls' words floated on top. I lay longer now, and deeper far; heavier weeds were falling on me. ...

"Come on, Loll. Time to go to bed. They boys went up long ago." The whispering girls bent over me; the kitchen returned upside down. "Wake up, lamb. ... He's whacked to the wide. Let's try and carry him up."

Half-waking, half-carried, they got me upstairs. I felt drunk and tattered with dreams. They dragged me stumbling round the bend in the landing, and then I smelt the sweet blankets of bed.

It was cold in the bedroom; there were no fires here. Jack lay open-mouthed, asleep. Shivering, I swayed while the girls undressed me, giggling around my buttons. They left me my shirt and my woollen socks, then stuffed me between the sheets.

Away went the candle down the stairs, boards creaked and the kitchen door shut. Darkness. Shapes returning slow. The window a square of silver. My bed-half was cold—Jack hot as a bird. For a while I lay doubled, teeth-chattering, blowing, warming against him slowly.

"Keep yer knees to yerself," said Jack, turning over. He woke. "Say, think of a number!"

"'Leven-hundred and two," I groaned, in a trance.

"Double it," he hissed in my ear.

Double it. . . . Twenny-four hundred and what? Can't do it. Something or other. . . . A dog barked again and swallowed a goose. The kitchen still murmured downstairs. Jack quickly submerged, having fired off his guns, and began snorkling away at my side. Gradually I straightened my rigid limbs and hooked all my fingers together. I felt wide awake now. I thought I'd count to a million. "One, two . . ." I said; that's all.

From *Cider With Rosie* (1959)

An Orphan Family

CAPT. MARRYAT

It is the time of the Civil War. Their mother dead, their father killed fighting for the King at the battle of Naseby, the four Beverley children are cared for by an elderly relative. One night a party of Roundhead troopers arrives at Arnwood, the Beverleys' family estate on the borders of the New Forest. They intend to burn the place down. Jacob Armitage, an old forester, is in time to rescue the four children, and take them into hiding in his own cottage deep in the forest. . . .

The old forester lay awake the whole of this night reflecting how he should act relative to the children; he felt the great responsibility he had incurred, and was alarmed when he considered what the consequences might be if his days were shortened. What would become of them—living in so sequestered a spot that few knew even of its existence—totally shut out from the world, and left to their own resources? He had no fear, if his life was spared, that they would do well; but if he should be called away before they had grown up and were unable to help themselves, they might perish. Edward was not fourteen years old. It was true that he was an active, brave boy, and thoughtful for his years; but he had not yet strength or skill sufficient for what would be required. Humphrey, the second, also promised well; but still they were all children. "I must bring them up to be useful, to depend upon themselves; there is not a moment to be lost, and not a moment shall be lost. I will do my best and trust to God. I ask but two or three years, and by that time I trust that they will be able to do without me. They must commence tomorrow the life of forester's children."

Acting upon this resolution, Jacob, as soon as the children were dressed and in the sitting-room, opened his Bible, which he had put on the table, and said,—

"My dear children, you know that you must remain in this cottage, that the wicked troopers may not find you out; they killed your father, and if I had not taken you away they would have burnt you in your beds. You must therefore live here as my children, and you must call yourselves by the name of Armitage, and not that of Beverley; and you must dress like children of the forest, and you must do as children of the forest do—that is, you must do everything for your-selves, for you can have no servants to wait upon you. We must all work; but you will like to work if you all work together, for then the work will be nothing but play. Now, Edward is the oldest, and he must go out with me in the forest, and I must teach him to kill deer and other game for our support; and when he knows how, then Humphrey shall come out and learn how to shoot; and sometimes I shall go by myself and leave Edward to work with you when there is work to be done. Alice, dear, you must, with Humphrey, light the fire and clean the house in the morning. Humphrey will go to the spring for water and do all the hard work; and you must learn to wash, my dear Alice—I will show you how; and you must learn to get dinner ready with Humphrey, who will assist you; and to make the beds. And little Edith shall take care of the fowls, and feed them every morning, and look for the eggs—will you, Edith?

"Yes," replied Edith, "and feed all the little chickens when they are hatched, as I did at Arnwood."

"Yes, dear; and you'll be very useful. Now you know that you cannot do all this at once. You will have to try and try again; but very soon you will, and then it will be all play. I must teach you all, and every day you will do it better, till you want no teaching at all. And now, my dear children, as there is no chaplain here, we must read the Bible every morning. Edward can read, I know; can you, Humphrey?'

"Yes, all except the big words."

"Well, you will learn them by-and-by. And Edward and I will teach Alice and Edith to read in the evenings, when we have nothing to do. It will be an amusement. Now, tell me, do you all like what I have told you?"

"Yes," they all replied; and then Jacob Armitage read a chapter in the Bible, after which they all knelt down and said the Lord's Prayer. . . . Jacob then showed them again how to clean the house, and Humphrey and Alice soon finished their work under his directions; and then they all sat down to breakfast, which was a very plain one, being generally cold meat, and cakes baked on the embers, at which Alice was soon very expert; and little Edith was very useful in watching them for her, while she busied herself about her other work. But the venison was nearly all gone; and after breakfast Jacob and Edward, with the dog Smoker, went out into the woods. Edward had no gun, as he only went out to be taught how to approach the game, which required great caution; indeed Jacob had no second gun to give him, if he had wished to do so.

"Now, Edward, we are going after a fine stag, if we can find him—which I doubt not—but the difficulty is to get within shot of him. Recollect that you must always be hid, for his sight is very quick; never be heard, for his ear is sharp; and never come down to him with the wind, for his scent is very fine. Then you must hunt according to the hour of the day. At this time he is feeding; two hours hence he will be lying down in the high fern. The dog is of no use unless the stag is badly wounded, when the dog will take him. Smoker knows his duty well, and will hide himself as close as we do. We are now going into the thick wood ahead of us, as there are many little spots of cleared ground in it where we may find the deer; but we must keep more to the left, for the wind is to the eastward, and we must walk up against it. And now that we are coming into the wood, recollect not a word must be said, and you must walk as quietly as possible, keeping behind me.—Smoker, to heel!" They proceeded through the wood for more than a mile, when Jacob made a sign to Edward and dropped down into the fern, crawling along to an open spot, where, at some distance, were a stag and three deer grazing. The deer grazed quietly, but the stag was ever and anon raising his head and snuffing the air as he looked around, evidently acting as a sentinel for the females.

The stag was perhaps a long quarter of a mile from where they were crouched down in the fern. Jacob remained immovable till the animal began to feed again, and then he advanced crawling through the fern, followed by Edward and the dog, who dragged himself on his stomach after Edward. This tedious approach was continued for some time, and they had neared the stag to within half the original distance, when the animal again lifted up his head and appeared uneasy. Jacob stopped and remained without motion. After a time the stag walked away, followed by the does, to the opposite side of the clear spot on which they had been feeding, and, to Edward's annoyance, the animal was now half a mile from them. Jacob turned round and crawled into the wood, and when he knew that they were concealed, he rose on to his feet and said,—

"You see, Edward, that it requires patience to stalk a deer. What a princely fellow! but he has probably been alarmed this morning, and is very uneasy. Now we must go through the woods till we come to the lee of him on the other side of the dell. You see he has led the does close to the thicket, and we shall have a better chance when we get there, if we are only quiet and cautious."

"What startled him, do you think?" said Edward.

"I think, when you were crawling through the fern after me, you broke a piece of rotten stick that was under you, did you not?"

"Yes, but that made but little noise."

"Quite enough to startle a red deer, Edward, as you will find out before you have been long a forester. These checks will happen, and have happened to me a hundred times, and then all the work is to be done over again. Now then to make a circuit—we had better not say a word. If we get safe now to the other side, we are sure of him."

They proceeded at a quick walk through the forest, and in half an hour had gained the side where the deer were feeding. . . . At last they came to the fern at the side of the wood, and crawled through it as before, but still more cautiously as they approached the stag. In this manner they arrived at last to within eighty yards of the animal, and then Jacob advanced his gun ready to put it to his shoulder, and as he cocked the lock, raised himself to fire. The click occasioned by the cocking of the lock roused up the stag instantly, and he turned his head in the direction from whence the noise proceeded. As he did so, Jacob fired, aiming behind the animal's shoulder; the stag made a bound, came down again, dropped on his knees, attempted to run, and fell dead, while the does fled with the rapidity of the wind.

Edward started up on his legs with a shout of exultation. Jacob commenced reloading his gun, and stopped Edward as he was about to run up to where the animal lay.

"Edward, you must learn your craft," said Jacob; "never do that again; never shout in that way. On the contrary, you should have remained still in the fern."

"Why so? the stag is dead."

"Yes, my dear boy, that stag is dead; but how do you know but what there may be another lying down in the fern close to us, or at some distance from us, which you have alarmed by your shout? Suppose that we both had had guns, and that the report of mine had started another stag lying in the fern within shot, you would have been able to shoot it; or if the stag was lying at a distance, the report of the gun might have startled him so as to induce him to move his head without rising. I should have seen his antlers move and marked his lair, and we should then have gone after him and stalked him, too."

"I see," replied Edward, "I was wrong; but I shall know better another time."

"That's why I tell you, my boy," replied Jacob; "now let us go to our quarry. Ay, Edward, this is a noble beast. I thought he was a hart royal, and so he is."

"What is a hart royal, Jacob?"

"Why, a stag is called a brocket until he is three years old; at four years he is a staggart; at five years a warrantable stag; and after five years he becomes a hart royal."

"And how do you know his age?"

"By his antlers. You see that this stag has nine antlers; now, a brocket has but two antlers, a staggart three, and a warrantable stag but four; at six years old the antlers increase in number until they sometimes have twenty or thirty. This is a fine beast, and the venison is now getting very good. Now you must see me do the work of my craft."

Jacob then cut the throat of the animal, and afterwards cut off its head, and took out its bowels.

"Are you tired, Edward?" said Jacob, as he wiped his hunting knife on the coat of the stag.

"No, not the least."

"Well, then, we are now, I should think, about four or five miles from the cottage. Could you find your way home? But that is of no consequence; Smoker will lead you home by the shortest path. I will stay here, and you can saddle White Billy and come back with him, for he must carry the venison back. It's more than we can manage—indeed, as much as we can manage with White Billy to help us. There's more than twenty stone of venison lying there, I can tell you."

Edward immediately assented, and Jacob, desiring Smoker to go home, set about flaying and cutting up the animal for its more convenient transportation. In an hour and a half, Edward, attended by Smoker, returned with the pony, on whose back the chief portion of the venison was packed. Jacob took a large piece on his shoulders, and Edward carried another, and Smoker, after regaling himself with a portion of the inside of the animal, came after them. During the walk home, Jacob initiated Edward into the terms of venery and many other points connected with deer-stalking ... As soon as they arrived at the cottage, the venison was hung up, the pony put in the stable, and they sat down to dinner with an excellent appetite after their long morning's walk. Alice and Humphrey had cooked the dinner themselves, and it was in the pot, smoking hot, when they returned; and Jacob declared he never ate a better mess in his life. Alice was not a little proud of this, and of the praises she received from Edward and the old forester.

(Next day, Jacob takes some of the venison to sell in Lymington, and buys a gun for Edward.)

Jacob ... returned late at night with White Billy well loaded: he had a sack of oatmeal, some spades and hoes, a saw and chisels, and other tools; two scythes and two three-pronged forks; and when Edward came to meet him, he put into his hand a gun with a very long barrel.

"I believe, Edward, that you will find that a good one, for I know where it came from. It belonged to one of the rangers, who was reckoned to be the best shot in the forest. I know the gun, for I have seen it on his arm, and have taken it in my hand to examine it, more than once. He was killed at Naseby, with your father, poor fellow! and his widow sold the gun to meet her wants."

"Well!" replied Edward, "I thank you much, Jacob, and I will try if I cannot kill as much venison as will pay back the purchase-money—I will, I assure you."

"I shall be glad if you do, Edward; not because I want the money back, but because then I shall be more easy in my mind about you all if anything happens to me. As soon as you are perfect in your woodcraft, I shall take Humphrey in hand, for there is nothing like having two strings to your bow.

To-morrow we will not go out: we have meat enough for three weeks or more; and now the frost has set in, it will keep well. You shall practise at a mark with your gun, that you may be accustomed to it; for all guns, even the best, require a little humouring."

Edward, who had often fired a gun before, proved the next morning that he had a very good eye, and after two or three hours' practice, hit the mark at a hundred yards almost every time.

"I wish you would let me go out by myself," said Edward, overjoyed by his success.

"You would bring home nothing, boy," replied Jacob. "No, no, you have a great deal to learn yet. But I tell you what you shall do: any time that we are not in great want of venison, you shall have the first fire."

"Well, that will do," replied Edward.

The winter now set in with great severity, and they remained almost altogether within doors. Jacob and the boys went out to get firewood, and dragged it home through the snow.

"I wish, Jacob," said Humphrey, "that I was able to build a cart, for it would be very useful, and White Billy would then have something to do; but I can't make the wheels, and there is no harness."

"That's not a bad idea of yours, Humphrey," replied Jacob; "we will think about it. If you can't build a cart, perhaps I can buy one. It would be useful if it were only to take the dung out of the yard on to the potato ground; for I have hitherto carried it out in baskets, and it's hard work."

"Yes, and we might saw the wood into billets, and carry it home in the cart instead of dragging it this way: my shoulder is quite sore with the rope, it cuts me so."

"Well, when the weather breaks up, I will see what I can

do, Humphrey; but just now the roads are so blocked up that I do not think we could get a cart from Lymington to the cottage, although we can a horse, perhaps."

But if they remained indoors during the inclement weather, they were not idle. Jacob took this opportunity to instruct the children in everything. Alice learnt how to wash and how to cook. It is true that sometimes she scalded herself a little, sometimes burnt her fingers; and other accidents did occur, from the articles employed being too heavy for them to lift by themselves; but practice and dexterity compensated for want of strength, and fewer accidents happened every day. Humphrey had his carpenter's tools; and although at first he had many failures, and wasted nails and wood, by degrees he learnt to use his tools with more dexterity, and made several useful little articles. Little Edith could now do something, for she made and baked all the oatmeal cakes, which saved Alice a good deal of time and trouble in watching them. It was astonishing how much the children could do now there was no one to do it for them, and they had daily instruction from Jacob.

In the evening Alice sat down with her needle and thread to mend the clothes. At first they were not very well done, but she improved every day.... thus the winter passed away so rapidly that, although they had been five months at the cottage, it did not appear as if they had been there as many weeks. All were happy and contented, with the exception, perhaps, of Edward, who had fits of gloominess, and occasionally showed signs of impatience as to what was passing in the world, of which he remained in ignorance.

From *Children of the New Forest* (1847)

A Fly-Away Family

J. M. BARRIE

The Darling family lives in London. Mr Darling is a rather ridiculous man, Mrs Darling lives up to her name, and their three children are Wendy, John and Michael. The most distinctive thing about the Darlings is the guardian of their nursery. Other children have starched Nannies, but the Darlings have Nana, a huge, clever, Newfoundland dog. Mr Darling is inclined to feel that this lets him down in the eyes of his neighbours. On the night described here, he has had a silly row with Nana, after playing her a disgusting trick, and has dragged her away and chained her up in the yard as if she were just any old dog. Mr and Mrs Darling then go out to dinner; but Mrs Darling is uneasy, for she suspects that the children have already been visited by Peter Pan, half boy, half sprite, who escaped from home almost as soon as he was born, to avoid the tedium of growing up.

For a moment after Mr and Mrs Darling left the house the night-lights by the beds of the three children continued to burn clearly. They were awfully nice little night-lights, and one cannot help wishing that they could have kept awake to see Peter; but Wendy's light blinked and gave such a yawn that the other two yawned also, and before they could close their mouths all the three went out.

There was another light in the room now, a thousand

times brighter than the night-lights, and in the time we have taken to say this, it had been in all the drawers in the nursery, looking for Peter's shadow, rummaged the wardrobe and turned every pocket inside out. It was not really a light; it made this light by flashing about so quickly, but when it came to rest for a second you saw it was a fairy, no longer than your hand, but still growing. It was a girl called Tinker Bell, exquisitely gowned in a skeleton leaf, cut low and square, through which her figure could be seen to the best advantage. She was slightly inclined to *embonpoint*.

A moment after the fairy's entrance the window was blown open by the breathing of the little stars, and Peter dropped in. He had carried Tinker Bell part of the way, and his hand was still messy with the fairy dust.

"Tinker Bell," he called softly, after making sure that the children were asleep, "Tink, where are you?" She was in a jug for the moment, and liking it extremely; she had never been in a jug before.

"Oh, do come out of that jug, and tell me, do you know where they put my shadow?"

The loveliest tinkle as of golden bells answered him. It is the fairy language. You ordinary children can never hear it, but if you were to hear it you would know that you had heard it once before.

Tink said that the shadow was in the big box. She meant the chest of drawers, and Peter jumped at the drawers, scattering their contents to the floor with both hands, as kings toss ha'pence to the crowd. In a moment he had recovered his shadow, and in his delight he forgot that he had shut Tinker Bell up in the drawer.

If he thought at all, but I don't believe he ever thought, it was that he and his shadow, when brought near each other, would join like drops of water; and when they did not he was appalled. He tried to stick it on with soap from the bathroom, but that also failed. A shudder passed through Peter, and he sat on the floor and cried.

His sobs woke Wendy, and she sat up in bed. She was not alarmed to see a stranger crying on the nursery floor; she was only pleasantly interested.

"Boy," she said courteously, "why are you crying?"

Peter could be exceedingly polite also, having learned the grand manner at fairy ceremonies, and he rose and bowed to her beautifully. She was much pleased, and bowed beautifully to him from the bed.

"What's your name?" he asked.

"Wendy Moira Angela Darling," she replied with some satisfaction. "What is your name?"

"Peter Pan."

She was already sure that he must be Peter, but it did seem a comparatively short name.

"Is that all?"

"Yes," he said rather sharply. He felt for the first time that it was a shortish name.

"I'm so sorry," said Wendy Moira Angela.

"It doesn't matter," Peter gulped.

She asked where he lived.

"Second to the right," said Peter, "and then straight on till morning."

"What a funny address!"

Peter had a sinking feeling. For the first time he felt that perhaps it was a funny address.

"No, it isn't," he said.

"I mean," Wendy said nicely, remembering that she was hostess, "is that what they put on the letters?"

He wished she had not mentioned letters.

"Don't get any letters," he said contemptuously.

"But your mother gets letters?"

"Don't have a mother," he said. Not only had he no mother, but he had not the slightest desire to have one. He thought them very over-rated persons. Wendy, however, felt at once that she was in the presence of a tragedy.

"O Peter, no wonder you were crying," she said, and got out of bed and ran to him.

"I wasn't crying about mothers," he said rather indignantly. "I was crying because I can't get my shadow to stick on. Besides, I wasn't crying."

"It has come off?"

"Yes."

Then Wendy saw the shadow on the floor, looking so draggled, and she was frightfully sorry for Peter. "How awful!" she said, but she could not help smiling when she saw that he had been trying to stick it on with soap. How exactly like a boy!

Fortunately she knew at once what to do. "It must be sewn on," she said, just a little patronizingly.

"What's sewn?" he asked.

"You're dreadfully ignorant."

"No, I'm not."

But she was exulting in his ignorance. "I shall sew it on for you, my little man," she said, though he was as tall as herself; and she got out her housewife, and sewed the shadow on to Peter's foot.

"I dare say it will hurt a little," she warned him.

"Oh, I shan't cry," said Peter, who was already of opinion that he had never cried in his life. And he clenched his teeth and did not cry; and soon his shadow was behaving properly, though still a little creased.

"Perhaps I should have ironed it," Wendy said thoughtfully; but Peter, boylike, was indifferent to appearances, and he was now jumping about in the wildest glee. Alas, he had already forgotten that he owed his bliss to Wendy. He thought he had attached the shadow himself. "How clever I am," he crowed rapturously, "oh, the cleverness of me!"

It is humiliating to have to confess that this conceit of Peter was one of his most fascinating qualities. To put it with brutal frankness, there never was a cockier boy.

But for the moment Wendy was shocked. "Your conceit," she exclaimed with frightful sarcasm; "of course I did nothing!"

"You did a little," Peter said carelessly, and continued to dance.

"A little!" she replied with hauteur; "if I am no use I can at least withdraw;" and she sprang in the most dignified way into bed and covered her face with the blankets.

To induce her to look up he pretended to be going away, and when this failed he sat on the end of the bed and tapped her gently with his foot. "Wendy," he said, "don't withdraw. I can't help crowing, Wendy, when I'm pleased with myself." Still she would not look up, though she was listening eagerly. "Wendy," he continued in a voice that no woman has ever yet been able to resist, "Wendy, one girl is more use than twenty boys."

Now Wendy was every inch a woman, though there were not very many inches, and she peeped out of the bedclothes.

"Do you really think so, Peter?"

"Yes, I do."

"I think it's perfectly sweet of you," she declared, "and I'll get up again;" and she sat with him on the side of the bed. She also said she would give him a kiss if he liked, but Peter did not know what she meant, and he held out his hand expectantly.

"Surely you know what a kiss is?" she asked, aghast.

"I shall know when you give it to me," he replied stiffly; and not to hurt his feelings she gave him a thimble.

"Now," said he, "shall I give you a kiss?" and she replied with a slight primness, "If you please." She made herself rather cheap by inclining her face towards him, but he merely dropped an acorn button into her hand; so she slowly returned her face to where it had been before, and said nicely that she would wear his kiss on the chain round her neck. It was lucky that she did put it on that chain, for it was afterwards to save her life.

When people in our set are introduced, it is customary for them to ask each other's age, and so Wendy, who always liked to do the correct thing, asked Peter how old he was. It was not really a happy question to ask him; it was like an examination paper that asks grammar, when what you want to be asked is Kings of England.

"I don't know," he replied uneasily, "but I am quite young." He really knew nothing about it; he had merely suspicions, but he said at a venture, "Wendy, I ran away the day I was born."

Wendy was quite surprised, but interested; and she indicated in the charming drawing-room manner, by a touch on her night-gown, that he could sit nearer her.

"It was because I heard father and mother," he explained in a low voice, "talking about what I was to be when I became a man." He was extraordinarily agitated now. "I don't want ever to be a man," he said with passion. "I want always to be a little boy and to have fun. So I ran away to Kensington Gardens and lived a long long time among the fairies."

She gave him a look of the most intense admiration, and he thought it was because he had run away, but it was really because he knew fairies. Wendy had lived such a home life that to know fairies struck her as quite delightful. She poured out questions about them, to his surprise, for they were rather a nuisance to him, getting in his way and so on, and indeed he sometimes had to give them a hiding. Still, he liked them on the whole, and he told her about the beginning of fairies.

"You see, Wendy, when the first baby laughed for the first time, its laugh broke into a thousand pieces, and they all went skipping about, and that was the beginning of fairies."

Tedious talk this, but being a stay-at-home she liked it.

"And so," he went on good-naturedly, "there ought to be one fairy for every boy and girl."

"Ought to be? Isn't there?"

"No. You see, children know such a lot now, they soon don't believe in fairies, and every time a child says, 'I don't believe in fairies,' there is a fairy somewhere that falls down dead."

Really, he thought they had now talked enough about fairies, and it struck him that Tinker Bell was keeping very quiet. "I can't think where she has gone to," he said, rising, and he called Tink by name. Wendy's heart went flutter with a sudden thrill.

"Peter," she cried, clutching him, "you don't mean to tell me that there is a fairy in this room!"

"She was here just now," he said a little impatiently. "You don't hear her, do you?" and they both listened.

"The only sound I hear," said Wendy, "is like a tinkle of bells."

"Well, that's Tink, that's the fairy language. I think I hear her too."

The sound came from the chest of drawers, and Peter made a merry face. No one could ever look quite so merry as Peter, and the loveliest of gurgles was his laugh. He had his first laugh still.

"Wendy," he whispered gleefully, "I do believe I shut her up in the drawer!"

He let poor Tink out of the drawer, and she flew about the nursery screaming with fury. "You shouldn't say such things," Peter retorted. "Of course I'm very sorry, but how could I know you were in the drawer?"

Wendy was not listening to him. "O Peter," she cried, "if she would only stand still and let me see her!"

"They hardly ever stand still," he said, but for one moment Wendy saw the romantic figure come to rest on the cuckoo clock. "O the lovely!" she cried, though Tink's face was still distorted with passion.

"Tink," said Peter amiably, "this lady says she wishes you were her fairy."

Tinker Bell answered insolently.

"What does she say, Peter?"

He had to translate. "She is not very polite. She says you are a great ugly girl, and that she is my fairy."

He tried to argue with Tink. "You know you can't be my fairy, Tink, because I am a gentleman and you are a lady."

To this Tink replied in these words, "You silly ass," and disappeared into the bathroom. "She is quite a common fairy," Peter explained apologetically; "she is called Tinker Bell because she mends the pots and kettles."

They were together in the arm-chair by this time, and Wendy plied him with more questions.

"If you don't live in Kensington Gardens now—"

"Sometimes I do still."

"But where do you live mostly now?"

"With the lost boys."

"Who are they?"

"They are the children who fall out of their perambulators when the nurse is looking the other way. If they are not claimed in seven days they are sent far away to the Neverland to defray expenses. I'm captain."

"What fun it must be!"

"Yes," said cunning Peter, "but we are rather lonely. You see we have no female companionship."

"Are none of the others girls?"

"Oh no; girls, you know, are much too clever to fall out of their prams."

This flattered Wendy immensely. "I think," she said, "it is perfectly lovely the way you talk about girls; John there just despises us."

For reply Peter rose and kicked John out of bed, blankets and all; one kick. This seemed to Wendy rather forward for a first meeting, and she told him with spirit that he was not captain in her house. However, John continued to sleep so placidly on the floor that she allowed him to remain there. "And I know you meant to be kind," she said, relenting, "so you may give me a kiss."

For a moment she had forgotten his ignorance about kisses. "I thought you would want it back," he said a little bitterly, and offered to return her the thimble.

"Oh dear," said the nice Wendy, "I don't mean a kiss, I mean a thimble."

"What's that?"

"It's like this." She kissed him.

"Funny!" said Peter gravely. "Now shall I give you a thimble?"

"If you wish to," said Wendy, keeping her head erect this time.

Peter thimbled her, and almost immediately she screeched.

"What is it, Wendy?"

"It was exactly as if someone were pulling my hair."

"That must have been Tink. I never knew her so naughty before."

And indeed Tink was darting about again, using offensive language.

"She says she will do that to you, Wendy, every time I give you a thimble."

"But why?"

"Why, Tink?"

Again Tink replied, "You silly ass." Peter could not understand why, but Wendy understood; and she was just slightly disappointed when he admitted that he came to the nursery window not to see her but to listen to stories.

"You see I don't know any stories. None of the lost boys know any stories."

"How perfectly awful," Wendy said.

"Do you know," Peter asked, "why swallows build in the eaves of houses? It is to listen to the stories. O Wendy, your mother was telling you such a lovely story."

"Which story was it?"

"About the prince who couldn't find the lady who wore the glass slipper."

"Peter," said Wendy excitedly, "that was Cinderella, and he found her, and they lived happy ever after."

Peter was so glad that he rose from the floor, where they had been sitting, and hurried to the window. "Where are you going?" she cried with misgiving.

"To tell the other boys."

"Don't go, Peter," she entreated, "I know such lots of stories."

Those were her precise words, so there can be no denying that it was she who first tempted him.

He came back, and there was a greedy look in his eyes now which ought to have alarmed her, but did not.

"Oh, the stories I could tell to the boys!" she cried, and then Peter gripped her and began to draw her towards the window.

"Let me go!" she ordered him.

"Wendy, do come with me and tell the other boys."

Of course she was very pleased to be asked, but she said, "Oh dear, I can't. Think of mummy! Besides, I can't fly."

"I'll teach you."

"Oh, how lovely to fly."

"I'll teach you how to jump on the wind's back, and then away we go."

"Oo!" she exclaimed rapturously.

"Wendy, Wendy, when you are sleeping in your silly bed you might be flying about with me saying funny things to the stars."

"Oo!"

"And, Wendy, there are mermaids."

"Mermaids! With tails?"

"Such long tails."

"Oh," cried Wendy, "to see a mermaid!"

He had become frightfully cunning. "Wendy," he said, "how we should all respect you."

She was wriggling her body in distress. It was quite as if she were trying to remain on the nursery floor.

But he had no pity for her.

"Wendy," he said, the sly one, "you could tuck us in at night."

"Oo!"

"None of us has ever been tucked in at night."

"Oo," and her arms went out to him.

"And you could darn our clothes, and make pockets for us.

None of us has any pockets."

How could she resist? "Of course it's awfully fascinating!" she cried. "Peter, would you teach John and Michael to fly too?"

"If you like," he said indifferently; and she ran to John and Michael and shook them. "Wake up," she cried, "Peter Pan has come and he is to teach us to fly."

John rubbed his eyes. "Then I shall get up," he said. Of course he was on the floor already. "Hallo," he said, "I am up!"

Michael was up by this time also, looking as sharp as a knife with six blades and a saw, but Peter suddenly signed silence. Their faces assumed the awful craftiness of children listening for sounds from the grown-up world. All was as still as salt. Then everything was right. No, stop! Everything was wrong. Nana, who had been barking distressfully all the evening, was quiet now. It was her silence they had heard.

"Out with the light! Hide! Quick!" cried John, taking command for the only time throughout the whole adventure. And thus when Liza entered, holding Nana, the nursery seemed quite its old self, very dark; and you could have sworn you heard its three wicked inmates breathing angelically as they slept. They were really doing it artfully from behind the window curtains.

Liza was in a bad temper, for she was mixing the Christmas puddings in the kitchen, and had been drawn away from them, with a raisin still on her cheek, by Nana's absurd suspicions. She thought the best way of getting a little quiet was to take Nana to the nursery for a moment, but in custody of course.

"There, you suspicious brute," she said, not sorry that Nana was in disgrace, "they are perfectly safe, aren't they?

Every one of the little angels sound asleep in bed. Listen to their gentle breathing."

Here Michael, encouraged by his success, breathed so loudly that they were nearly detected. Nana knew that kind of breathing, and she tried to drag herself out of Liza's clutches.

But Liza was dense. "No more of it, Nana," she said sternly, pulling her out of the room. "I warn you if you bark again I shall go straight for master and missus and bring them home from the party, and then, oh, won't master whip you, just."

She tied the unhappy dog up again, but do you think Nana ceased to bark? Bring master and missus home from the party! Why, that was just what she wanted. Do you think she cared whether she was whipped so long as her charges were safe? Unfortunately Liza returned to her puddings, and Nana, seeing that no help would come from her, strained and strained at the chain until at last she broke it. In another moment she had burst into the dining room of 27 and flung up her paws to heaven, her most expressive way of making a communication. Mr and Mrs Darling knew at once that something terrible was happening in their nursery, and without a good-bye to their hostess they rushed into the street.

But it was now ten minutes since three scoundrels had been breathing behind the curtains; and Peter Pan can do a great deal in ten minutes.

We now return to the nursery.

"It's all right," John announced, emerging from his hiding-place. "I say, Peter, can you really fly?"

Instead of troubling to answer him Peter flew round the room, taking in the mantelpiece on the way.

"How topping!" said John and Michael.

"How sweet!" cried Wendy.

"Yes, I'm sweet, oh, I am sweet!" said Peter, forgetting his manners again.

It looked delightfully easy, and they tried it first from the floor and then from the beds, but they always went down instead of up.

"I say, how do you do it?" asked John, rubbing his knee. He was quite a practical boy.

"You just think lovely wonderful thoughts," Peter explained, "and they lift you up in the air."

He showed them again.

"You're so nippy at it," John said; "couldn't you do it very slowly once?"

Peter did it both slowly and quickly. "I've got it now, Wendy!" cried John, but soon he found he had not. Not one of them could fly an inch, though even Michael was in words of two syllables, and Peter did not know A from Z.

Of course Peter had been trifling with them, for no one can fly unless the fairy dust has been blown on him. Fortunately, as we have mentioned, one of his hands was messy with it, and he blew some on each of them, with the most superb results.

"Now just wriggle your shoulders this way," he said, "and let go."

They were all on their beds, and gallant Michael let go first. He did not quite mean to let go, but he did it, and immediately he was borne across the room.

"I flewed!" he screamed while still in mid-air.

John let go and met Wendy near the bathroom.

"Oh, lovely!"

"Oh, ripping!"

"Look at me!"

"Look at me!"

"Look at me!"

They were not nearly so elegant as Peter, they could not help kicking a little, but their heads were bobbing against the ceiling, and there is almost nothing so delicious as that. Peter gave Wendy a hand at first, but had to desist, Tink was so indignant.

Up and down they went, and round and round. Heavenly was Wendy's word.

"I say," cried John, "why shouldn't we all go out!"

Of course it was to this that Peter had been luring them.

Michael was ready: he wanted to see how long it took him to do a billion miles. But Wendy hesitated.

"Mermaids!" said Peter again.

"Oo!"

"And there are pirates."

"Pirates," cried John, seizing his Sunday hat, "let us go at once."

It was just at this moment that Mr and Mrs Darling hurried with Nana out of 27. They ran into the middle of the street to look up at the nursery window; and, yes, it was still shut, but the room was ablaze with light, and most heart-gripping sight of all, they could see in shadow on the curtain three little figures in night attire circling round and round, not on the floor but in the air.

Not three figures, four!

In a tremble they opened the street door. Mr Darling would have rushed upstairs, but Mrs Darling signed to him to go softly. She even tried to make her heart go softly.

Will they reach the nursery in time? If so, how delightful for them, and we shall all breathe a sigh of relief, but there will be no story. On the other hand, if they are not in time, I solemnly promise that it will all come right in the end.

They would have reached the nursery in time had it not been that the little stars were watching them. Once again the stars blew the window open, and that smallest star of all called out:

"Cave, Peter!"

Then Peter knew that there was not a moment to lose. "Come," he cried imperiously, and soared out at once into the night followed by John and Michael and Wendy.

Mr and Mrs Darling and Nana rushed into the nursery too late. The birds were flown.

From *Peter Pan* (1911)

The Changeling

ANON

A changeling came about my house
And pressed her cheek against the pane,
And called me "Mother!" once and twice,
And called me "Mother!" thrice again.
    "Ah, Mother, Mother, let me bide—
    The wind is chill, the world is wide,
    Ah, Mother, let me come inside—
    Ah, Mother, Mother, let me in!"

Without a thought but only fear
I shot the bolt, the lattice slammed—
"I cannot let you come within,
My heart is full, my house is crammed:
  "There's three sleeps in the ingle
  And two that keeps the door,
  The girls are in the garret
  And in the loft two more.
  At dawn I blow the ashes,
  At noon I stir the pot,
  I push the door at almost four
  And rock the baby's cot.
  At five I hear them homing,
  At six I slice the bread,
  At half-past eight it's getting late—
  I hustle them to bed.
"This is the way my life goes,
And little need I rue—
Unless I open up my house
To take in such as you."
When many springs had passed my house
And pressed against the window pane,
That changeling came up to the sill
And whispered "Mother!" once again.
  "Ah, Mother, how are things with you?
  And have you tasted bitter rue
  As once you swore you'd never do?
  And how fare all who dwell within?

"I'll tell you how my life goes,
Now I break bitter bread,
And shall do till the day ends
And I lie stiff in bed:
　　"Two boys have gone a-sailing,
　　Two girls have gone to town,
　　Another lad's in prison
　　And another I saw drown;
　　The baby died of fever,
　　The twins went to the wars,
　　The seventh boy, a child of joy,
　　I turnèd out of doors.
　　I have none left to work for,
　　At dawn, at noon I mourn—
　　An empty cot is all I've got
　　And weeds grow on the lawn.
"Yes, this is how my life goes
That once was full of pride."
"Ah, Mother, Mother, Mother!"
"My darling—come inside!"

The Lumber-Room

"SAKI"

"Saki" was the pen name of H. H. Munro, who wrote short stories by the score in the years leading up to the first world war. He wrote of an England of men-about-town, country visits, thin bread-and-butter—and aunts. In those days there were a lot of aunts about. Unmarried daughters rapidly grew into aunts and found themselves caring for the children of brothers and sisters who had either died or were busy building the British Empire in remote parts of the world unhealthy for the young. Another writer has spoken of the "appalling auntly regime" of Saki's childhood. He gets his own back on aunts in his short stories.

The children were to be driven, as a special treat, to the sands at Jagborough. Nicholas was not to be of the party; he was in disgrace. Only that morning he had refused to eat his wholesome bread-and-milk on the seemingly frivolous ground that there was a frog in it. Older and wiser and better people had told him that there could not possibly be a frog in his bread-and-milk and that he was not to talk nonsense; he continued, nevertheless, to talk what seemed the veriest nonsense, and described with much detail the colouration and markings of the alleged frog. The dramatic part of the incident was that there really was a frog in Nicholas' basin of bread-and-milk; he had put it there himself, so he felt entitled to know something about it. The sin of taking a frog from the garden and putting it into a bowl of wholesome bread-and-milk was enlarged on at great length, but the fact that stood out clearest in the whole affair, as it presented itself to the mind of Nicholas, was that the older, wiser, and better people had been proved to be profoundly in error in matters about which they had expressed the utmost assurance.

"You said there couldn't possibly be a frog in my bread-and-milk; there *was* a frog in my bread-and-milk," he repeated, with the insistence of a skilled tactician who does not intend to shift from favourable ground.

So his boy-cousin and girl-cousin and his quite uninteresting younger brother were to be taken to Jagborough sands that afternoon and he was to stay at home. His cousins' aunt, who insisted, by an unwarranted stretch of imagination, in styling herself his aunt also, had hastily invented the Jagborough expedition in order to impress on Nicholas the delights that he had justly forfeited by his disgraceful conduct at the breakfast-table. It was her habit, whenever one of the children fell from grace, to improvise something of a festival nature from which the offender would be rigorously debarred; if all the children sinned collectively they were suddenly informed of a circus in the neighbouring town, a circus of unrivalled merit and uncounted elephants, to which, but for their depravity, they would have been taken that very day.

A few decent tears were looked for on the part of Nicholas when the moment for the departure of the expedition arrived. As a matter of fact, however, all the crying was done by his girl-cousin, who scraped her knee rather painfully against the step of the carriage as she was scrambling in.

"How she did howl," said Nicholas cheerfully, as the party drove off without any of the elation of high spirits that should have characterized it.

"She'll soon get over that," said the *soi-disant* aunt; "it will be a glorious afternoon for racing about over those beautiful sands. How they will enjoy themselves!"

"Bobby won't enjoy himself much, and he won't race much either," said Nicholas with a grim chuckle; "his boots are hurting him. They're too tight."

"Why didn't he tell me they were hurting?" asked the aunt with some asperity.

"He told you twice, but you weren't listening. You often don't listen when we tell you important things."

"You are not to go into the gooseberry garden," said the aunt, changing the subject.

"Why not?" demanded Nicholas.

"Because you are in disgrace," said the aunt loftily.

Nicholas did not admit the flawlessness of the reasoning; he felt perfectly capable of being in disgrace and in a gooseberry garden at the same moment. His face took on an expression of considerable obstinacy. It was clear to his aunt that he was determined to get into the gooseberry garden, "only," as she remarked to herself, "because I have told him he is not to."

Now the gooseberry garden had two doors by which it might be entered, and once a small person like Nicholas could slip in there he could effectually disappear from view amid the masking growth of artichokes, raspberry canes, and fruit bushes. The aunt had many other things to do that afternoon, but she spent an hour or two in trivial gardening operations among flower beds and shrubberies, whence she could keep a watchful eye on the two doors that led to the forbidden paradise. She was a woman of few ideas, with immense powers of concentration.

Nicholas made one or two sorties into the front garden, wriggling his way with obvious stealth of purpose towards one or other of the doors, but never able for a moment to evade the aunt's watchful eye. As a matter of fact, he had no intention of trying to get into the gooseberry garden, but it was extremely convenient for him that his aunt should believe that he had; it was a belief that would keep her on self-imposed sentry-duty for the greater part of the afternoon. Having thoroughly confirmed and fortified her suspicions, Nicholas slipped back into the house and rapidly put into execution a plan of action that had long germinated in his brain. By standing on a chair in the library one could reach a shelf on which reposed a fat, important-looking key. The key was as important as it looked; it was the instrument which kept the mysteries of the lumber-room secure from unauthorized intrusion, which opened a way only for aunts and such-like privileged persons. Nicholas had not had much experience of the art of fitting keys into keyholes and turning locks, but for some days past he had practised with the key of the schoolroom door; he did not believe in trusting too much to luck and accident. The key turned stiffly in the lock, but it turned. The door opened, and Nicholas was in an unknown land, compared with which the gooseberry garden was a stale delight, a mere material pleasure.

Often and often Nicholas had pictured to himself what the lumber-room might be like, that region that was so carefully sealed from youthful eyes and concerning which no questions were ever answered. It came up to his expectations. In the first place it was large and dimly lit, one high window opening on to the forbidden garden being its only source of illumination. In the second place it was a storehouse of unimagined treasures. The aunt-by-assertion was one of those people who think that things spoil by use and consign them to dust and damp by way of preserving them. Such parts of the house as Nicholas knew best were rather bare and cheerless, but here

there were wonderful things for the eye to feast on. First and foremost there was a piece of framed tapestry that was evidently meant to be a fire-screen. To Nicholas it was a living, breathing story; he sat down on a roll of Indian hangings, glowing in wonderful colours beneath a layer of dust, and took in all the details of the tapestry picture. A man, dressed in the hunting costume of some remote period, had just transfixed a stag with an arrow; it could not have been a difficult shot because the stag was only one or two paces away from him; in the thickly growing vegetation that the picture suggested it would not have been difficult to creep up to a feeding stag, and the two spotted dogs that were springing forward to join in the chase had evidently been trained to keep to heel till the arrow was discharged. That part of the picture was simple, if interesting, but did the huntsman see, what Nicholas saw, that four galloping wolves were coming in his direction through the wood? There might be more than four of them hidden behind the trees, and in any case would the man and his dogs be able to cope with the four wolves if they made an attack? The man had only two arrows left in his quiver, and he might miss with one or both of them; all one knew about his skill in shooting was that he could hit a large stag at a ridiculously short range. Nicholas sat for many golden minutes revolving the possibilities of the scene; he was inclined to think that there were more than four wolves and that the man and his dogs were in a tight corner.

But there were other objects of delight and interest claiming his instant attention: there were quaint twisted candlesticks in the shape of snakes, and a teapot fashioned like a china duck, out of whose open beak the tea was supposed to come. How dull and shapeless the nursery teapot seemed in comparison! And there was a carved sandal-wood box packed tight with aromatic cotton-wool, and between the layers of cotton-wool were little brass figures, hump-necked bulls, and peacocks and goblins, delightful to see and to handle. Less promising in appearance was a large square book with plain black covers; Nicholas peeped into it, and, behold, it was full of coloured pictures of birds. And such birds! In the garden, and in the lanes when he went for a walk, Nicholas came across a few birds, of which the largest were an occasional magpie or wood-pigeon; here were herons and bustards, kites, toucans, tiger-bitterns, bush turkeys, ibises, golden pheasants, a whole portrait gallery of undreamed-of creatures. And as he was admiring the colouring of the mandarin duck and assigning a life-history to it, the voice of his aunt in shrill vociferation of his name came from the gooseberry garden without. She had grown suspicious at his long disappearance, and had leapt to the conclusion that he had climbed over the wall behind the sheltering screen of the lilac bushes; she was now engaged in energetic and rather hopeless search for him among the artichokes and raspberry canes.

"Nicholas, Nicholas!" she screamed, "you are to come out of this at once. It's no use trying to hide there; I can see you all the time."

It was probably the first time for twenty years that any one had smiled in that lumber-room.

Presently the angry repetitions of Nicholas' name gave way to a shriek, and a cry for somebody to come quickly. Nicholas shut the book, restored it carefully to its place in a corner, and shook some dust from a neighbouring pile of newspapers over it. Then he crept from the room, locked the door, and replaced the key exactly where he had found it. His aunt was still calling his name when he sauntered into the front garden.

"Who's calling?" he asked.

"Me," came the answer from the other side of the wall; "didn't you hear me? I've been looking for you in the gooseberry garden, and I've slipped into the rain-water tank. Luckily there's no water in it, but the sides are slippery and I can't get out. Fetch the ladder from under the cherry tree—"

"I was told I wasn't to go into the gooseberry garden," said Nicholas promptly.

"I told you not to, and now I tell you that you may," came the voice from the rain-water tank, rather impatiently.

"Your voice doesn't sound like aunt's," objected Nicholas; "you may be the Evil One tempting me to be disobedient. Aunt often tells me that the Evil One tempts me and that I always yield. This time I'm not going to yield."

"Don't talk nonsense," said the prisoner in the tank; "go and fetch the ladder."

"Will there be strawberry jam for tea?" asked Nicholas innocently.

"Certainly there will be," said the aunt, privately resolving that Nicholas should have none of it.

"Now I know that you are the Evil One and not aunt," shouted Nicholas gleefully; "when we asked aunt for strawberry jam yesterday she said there wasn't any. I know there are four jars of it in the store cupboard, because I looked, and of course you know it's there, but *she* doesn't, because she said there wasn't any. Oh, Devil, you *have* sold yourself!"

There was an unusual sense of luxury in being able to talk to an aunt as though one was talking to the Evil One, but Nicholas knew, with childish discernment, that such luxuries were not to be over-indulged in. He walked noisily away, and it was a kitchenmaid, in search of parsley, who eventually rescued the aunt from the rain-water tank.

Tea that evening was partaken of in a fearsome silence. The tide had been at its highest when the children had arrived at Jagborough Cove, so there had been no sands to play on—a circumstance the aunt had overlooked in the haste of organizing her punitive expedition. The tightness of Bobby's boots had had disastrous effect on his temper the whole of the afternoon, and altogether the children could not have been said to have enjoyed themselves. The aunt maintained the frozen muteness of one who has suffered un-dignified and unmerited detention in a rain-water tank for thirty-five minutes. As for Nicholas, he, too, was silent, in the absorption of one who has much to think about; it was just possible, he considered, that the huntsman would escape with his hounds while the wolves feasted on the stricken stag.

The General Sees Active Service

ETHEL TURNER

There was another book about these seven children, called The Family At
Misrule, *but in the present story their mother is dead, they have a kind but rather
silly stepmother, and their father is a most appalling bully. He is always called*
The Captain, *which may be why the baby is called by his brothers and sisters*
The General. *A misdemeanour in the previous chapter has deprived the children
of an outing. But they cannot keep out of trouble—which is amply demonstrated
in this extract:—*

It was a day after "the events narrated in the last chapter,"
as story-book parlance has it. And Judy, with a wrathful look
in her eyes, was sitting on the nursery table, her knees touching her chin and her thin brown hands clasped round them.

"It's a shame," she said, "it's a burning, wicked shame!
What's the use of fathers in the world, I'd like to know!"

"Oh, Judy!" said Meg, who was curled up in an armchair,
deep in a book. But she said it mechanically, and only as a
matter of duty, being three years older than Judy.

"Think of the times we could have if he didn't live with
us," Judy continued, calmly disregardful. "Why, we'd have
fowl three times a day, and the pantomime seven nights a
week."

Nell suggested that it was not quite usual to have panto-mimic performances on the seventh day, but Judy was not daunted.

"I'd have a kind of church pantomime," she said thought-fully,—"beautiful pictures and things about the Holy Land, and the loveliest music, and beautiful children in white sing-ing hymns, and bright colours all about, and no collection plates to take your only threepenny bit—oh! and no sermons or litanies, of course."

"Oh, Judy!" murmured Meg, turning a leaf.

Judy unclasped her hands, and then clasped them again more tightly than before. "Six whole tickets wasted—thirty beautiful shillings—just because we have a father!"

"He sent them to the Digby-Smiths," Bunty volunteered, "and wrote on the envelope, '*With Compts.*—J. C. Wool-cot.'"

Judy moaned. "Six horrid little Digby-Smiths sitting in the theatre watching our fun with their six horrid little eyes," she said bitterly.

Bunty, who was mathematically inclined, wanted to know why they wouldn't look at it through their twelve horrid little eyes, and Judy laughed and came down from the table, after expressing a wicked wish that the little Digby-Smiths might all tumble over the dress circle rail before the curtain rose. Meg shut her book with a hurried bang.

"Has Pip gone yet? Father'll be awfully cross. Oh *dear*, what a head I've got!" she said. "Where's Esther? has anyone seen Esther?"

"My *dear* Meg!" Judy said; "why, it's at least two hours since Esther went up the drive before your very nose. She's gone to Waverly,—why, she came in and told you, and said she trusted you to see about the coat, and you said, ''M—'m! all right.'"

Meg gave a startled look of recollection. "Did I have to clean it?" she asked in a frightened tone, and pushing her fair hair back from her forehead. "Oh, girls! what *was* it I had to do?"

"Clean with benzine, iron while wet, put in a cool place to keep warm, and bake till brown," said Judy promptly. "*Surely* you heard, Margaret? Esther was at such pains to explain."

Meg ruffled her hair again despairingly. "What shall I do?" she said, actual tears springing to her eyes. "What will father say? Oh, Judy, you might have reminded me."

Nell slipped an arm round her neck. "She's only teasing, Megsie; Esther did it and left it ready in the hall—you've only to give it to Pip. Pat has to take the dogcart into town this afternoon to have the back seat mended, and Pip's going in it too, that's all, and they're putting the horse in now; you're not late."

It was the coat Bunty had done his best to spoil that all the trouble was about. It belonged, as I said, to the Captain's full-dress uniform, and was wanted for a dinner at the Barracks this same evening. And Esther had been sponging and cleaning at it all the morning, and had left directions that it was to be taken to the Barracks in the afternoon.

Presently the dogcart came spinning round to the door in great style, Pip driving and Pat looking sulkily on. They took the coat parcel and put it carefully under the seat, and were preparing to start again, when Judy came out upon the verandah, holding the General in an uncomfortable position in her arms.

"You come too, Fizz, there's heaps of room,—there's no reason you shouldn't," Pip said suddenly.

"Oh—h—h!" said Judy, her eyes sparkling. She took a rapid step forward and lifted her foot to get in.

"Oh, I say!" remonstrated Pip, "you'll have to put on something over that dress, old girl,—it's all over jam and things."

Judy shot herself into the hall and returned with her ulster; she set the General on the floor for a minute while she donned it, then picked him up and handed him up to Pip.

"He'll have to come too," she said; "I promised Esther I wouldn't let him out of my sight for a minute; she's getting quite nervous about him lately,—thinks he'll get broken."

Pip grumbled a minute or two, but the General gave a gurgling, captivating laugh and held up his arms, so he took him up and held him while Judy clambered in.

"We can come back in the tram to the Quay, and then get a boat back," she said, squeezing the baby on the seat between them. "The General loves going on the water."

Away they sped; down the neglected carriage drive, out of the gates, and away down the road, Pip, Judy of the shining eyes, the General devouring his thumb, and Pat smiling-faced once more because in possession of the reins.

A wind from the river swept through the belt of gum trees on the Crown lands, and sent the young red blood leaping through their veins; it played havoc with Judy's curls, and dyed her brown cheeks a warm red; it made the General kick and laugh and grow restive, and caused Pip to stick his hat on the back of his head and whistle joyously.

Until town was reached, when they were forced to yield somewhat to the claims of conventionality.

On the way to Paddington a gentleman on horseback slackened pace a little. Pip took off his hat with a flourish, and Judy gave a frank, pleased smile, for it was a certain old Colonel they had known for years, and had cause to remember his good-humour and liberality.

"Well, my little maid,—well, Philip, lad," he said, smiling

genially, while his horse danced round the dogcart,—"and the General too,—where are you all off to?"

"The Barracks,—I'm taking something up for the governor," Pip answered. Judy was watching the plunging horse with admiring eyes. "And then we're going back home."

The old gentleman managed, in spite of the horse's tricks, to slip his hand in his pocket. "Here's something to make yourselves ill with on the way," he said, handing them two half-crowns; "but don't send me the doctor's bill."

He flicked the General's cheek with his whip, gave Judy a nod, and cantered off.

The children looked at each other with sparkling eyes.

"Cocoanuts," Pip said, "and tarts and toffee, and save the rest for a football?" Judy shook her head.

"Where do *I* come in?" she said. "You'd keep the football at school. I vote pink jujubes, and icecreams, and a wax doll."

"A wax grandmother!" Pip retorted; "you wouldn't be such a girl, I hope." Then he added, with almost pious fervour, "Thank goodness you've always hated dolls, Fizz."

Judy gave a sudden leap in her seat, almost upsetting the General, and bringing down upon her head a storm of reproaches from the coachman. "*I* know!" she said; "and we're almost half way there now. Oh—h—h! it *will* be lovely."

Pip urged her to explain herself.

"Bondi Aquarium,—skating, boats, merry-go-round, switchback threepence a go!" she returned succinctly.

"Good iron," Pip whistled softly, while he revolved the thing in his mind. "There'd be something over, too, to get some tucker with, and perhaps something for the football too." Then his brow clouded.

"There's the kid,—whatever did you go bringing him for?

Just like a girl, to spoil everything!"

Judy looked nonplussed. "I quite forgot him," she said, vexedly. "Couldn't we leave him somewhere? couldn't we ask someone to take care of him while we go? Oh, it would be *too* bad to have to give it up just because of him. It's beginning to rain, too; we couldn't take him with us."

They were at the foot of Barrack Hill now, and Pat told them they must get out and walk the rest of the way up, or he would never get the dogcart finished to take back that evening.

Pip tumbled out and took the General, all in a bunched-up heap, and Judy alighted carefully after him, the precious coat parcel in her arms. And they walked up the asphalt hill to the gate leading to the officer's quarters in utter silence.

"Well?" Pip said querulously, as they reached the top. "Be quick; haven't you thought of anything?"

That levelling of brows, and pursing of lips, always meant deep and intricate calculation on his sister's part, as he knew full well.

"Yes," Judy said quietly. "I've got a plan that will do, I think." Then a sudden fire entered her manner.

"Who is the General's father? tell me that," she said in a rapid, eager way; "and isn't it right and proper fathers should look after their sons? and doesn't he deserve we should get even with him for doing us out of the pantomime? and isn't the Aquarium too lovely to miss?"

"Well?" Pip said; his slower brain did not follow such rapid reasoning.

"Only I'm going to leave the General here at the Barracks for a couple of hours till we come back, his father being the proper person to watch over him." Judy grasped the General's small fat hand in a determined way, and opened the gate.

"Oh, I say," remarked Pip, "we'll get in an awful row, you know, Fizz. I don't think we'd better,—I don't really, old girl."

"Not a bit," said Judy stoutly—"at least, only a bit, and the Aquarium's worth that. Look how it's raining; the child will get croup, or rheumatism, or something if we take him; there's father standing over on the green near the tennis-court talking to a man. I'll slip quietly along the verandah, and into his own room, and put the coat and the General on the bed; then I'll tell a soldier to go and tell father his parcels have come, and while he's gone I'll fly back to you, and we'll catch the tram and go to the Aquarium."

Pip whistled again, softly. He was used to bold proposals from this sister of his, but this was beyond everything. "B—b—but," he said uneasily, "but, Judy, whatever would he do with that kid for two mortal hours?"

"Mind him," Judy returned promptly. "It's a pretty thing if a father can't mind his own child for two hours. Afterwards, you see, when we've been to the Aquarium, we will come back and fetch him, and we can explain to father how it was raining, and that we thought we'd better not take him with us for fear of rheumatism, and that we were in a hurry to catch the tram, and as he wasn't in his room we just put him on the bed till he came. Why, Pip, it's beautifully simple!"

Pip still looked uncomfortable. "I don't like it, Fizz," he said again; "he'll be in a fearful wax."

Judy gave him one exasperated look. "Go and see if that's the Bondi tram coming," she said; and, glad of a moment's respite, he went down the path again to the pavement and looked down the hill. When he turned round again she had gone.

He stuck his hands in his pockets and walked up and down

the path a few times. "Fizz'll get us hanged yet," he muttered, looking darkly at the door in the wall through which she had disappeared.

He pushed his hat to the back of his head and stared gloomily at his boots, wondering what would be the consequences of this new mischief. There was a light footfall beside him.

"Come on," said Judy, pulling his sleeve; "it's done now, come on, let's go and have our fun; have you got the money safe?"

It was two o'clock as they passed out of the gate and turned their faces up the hill to the tram stopping-place. And it was half-past four when they jumped out of a town-bound tram and entered the gates again to pick up their charge.

Such an afternoon as they had had! Once inside the Aquarium, even Pip had put his conscience qualms on one side, and bent all his energies to enjoying himself thoroughly. And Judy was like a little mad thing. She spent a shilling of her money on the switchback railway, pronouncing the swift, bewildering motion "heavenly". The first journey made Pip feel sick, so he eschewed a repetition of it, and watched Judy go off from time to time, waving gaily from the perilous little car, almost with his heart in his mouth. Then they hired a pair of roller skates each, and bruised themselves black and blue with heavy falls on the asphalt. After that they had a ride on the merry-go-round, but Judy found it tame after the switch-back, and refused to squander a second threepence upon it, contenting herself with watching Pip fly round, and madly running by his side to keep up as long as she could. They finished the afternoon with a prolonged inspection of the fish-tanks, a light repast of jam tarts of questionable freshness, and two-pennyworth of peanuts. And, as I said, it was half-past four as they hastened up the path again to the top gate of the Barracks.

"I *hope* he's been good," Judy said, as she turned the handle. "Yes, you come too, Pip,"—for that young gentleman hung back one agonised second. "Twenty kicks or blows divided by two only make ten, you see."

They went up the long stone verandah and stopped at one door.

There was a little knot of young officers laughing and talking close by.

"Take my word, 'twas as good as a play to see Wooly grabbing his youngster, and stuffing it into a cab, and getting in himself, all with a look of ponderous injured dignity," one said, and laughed at the recollection.

Another blew away a cloud of cigar smoke. "It was a jolly little beggar," he said. "It doubled its fists and landed His High Mightiness one in the eye; and then its shoe dropped off, and we all rushed to pick it up, and it was muddy and generally dilapidated, and old Wooly went red slowly up to his ear-tips as he tried to put it on."

A little figure stepped into the middle of the group—a little figure with an impossibly short and shabby ulster, thin black-stockinged legs, and a big hat crushed over a tangle of curls.

"It is my father you are speaking of," she said, her head very high, her tone haughty, "and I cannot tell where your amusement is. Is my father here, or did I hear you say he had gone away?"

Two of the men looked a little foolish, the third took off his cap.

"I am sorry you should have overheard us, Miss Woolcot," he said pleasantly. "Still, there is no irreparable harm done, is there? Yes, your father has gone away in a cab. He couldn't imagine how the little boy came on his bed, and, as he couldn't keep him here very well, I suppose he has taken him home."

Something like a look of shame came into Judy's bright eyes.

"I am afraid I must have put my father to some inconvenience," she said quietly. "It was I who left the Gen—my brother here, because I didn't know what to do with him for an hour or two. But I quite meant to take him home myself. Has he been gone long?"

"About half an hour," the officer said, and tried not to look amused at the little girl's old-fashioned manner.

"Ah, thank you. Perhaps we can catch him up. Come on, Pip," and nodding in a grave, distant manner, she turned away, and went down the verandah and through the gate with her brother.

"A nice hole we're in," he said.

Judy nodded.

"It's about the very awfullest thing we've ever done in our lives. Fancy the governor carting that child all the way from here! Oh lor'!"

Judy nodded again.

"Can't you speak?" he said irritably. "You've got us into this—I didn't want to do it; but I'll stand by you, of course. Only you'll have to think of something quick."

Judy bit three finger-tips off her right-hand glove, and looked melancholy.

"There's absolutely nothing to do, Pip," she said slowly. "I didn't think it would turn out like this. I suppose we'd better just go straight back and hand ourselves over for punishment. He'll be too angry to hear any sort of an excuse, so we'd better just grin and bear whatever he does to us. I'm really sorry too that I made a laughing-stock of him up there."

Pip was explosive. He called her a little ass and a gowk and a stupid idiot for doing such a thing, and she did not reproach him or answer back once.

They caught a tram and went into Sydney, and afterwards to the boat. They ensconced themselves in a corner at the far end, and discussed the state of affairs with much seriousness. Then Pip got up and strolled about a little to relieve his feelings, coming back in a second with a white, scared face.

"He's on the boat," he said, in a horrified whisper.

"Where—where—where? what—what—what?" Judy cried unintentionally mimicking a long-buried monarch.

"In the cabin, looking as glum as a boiled wallaby, and hanging on to the poor little General as if he thinks he'll fly away."

Judy looked a little frightened for the first time.

"Can't we hide? Don't let's let him see us. It wouldn't be any good offering to take the General now. We're in for it now, Pip—there'll be no quarter."

Pip groaned; then Judy stood up.

"Let's creep down as far as the engine," she said, "and see if he does look very bad."

They made their way cautiously along the deck, and took up a position where they could see without being seen. The dear little General was sitting on the seat next to his stern father, who had a firm hold of the back of his woolly pelisse. He was sucking at his little dirty hand, and casting occasional longing glances at his tan shoe, which he knew was delicious to bite. Once or twice he had pulled it off and conveyed it to his mouth, but his father intercepted it, and angrily buttoned it on again in its rightful place. He wanted, too, to slither off the horrid seat, and crawl all over the deck, and explore the ground under the seats, and see where the puffing noise came from; but there was that iron grasp on his coat that no amount of wriggling would move. No wonder the poor child looked unhappy!

At last the boat stopped at a wharf not far from Misrule, and the Captain alighted, carrying his small dirty son gingerly in his arms. He walked slowly up the red road along which the dogcart had sped so blithesomely some six or seven hours ago, and Judy and Pip followed at a respectful—a very respectful—distance. At the gate he saw them, and gave a large, angry beckon for them to come up. Judy went very white, but obeyed instantly, and Pip, pulling himself together, brought up the rear.

Afterwards Judy only had a very indistinct remembrance of what happened during the next half-hour. She knew there was a stormy scene, in which Esther and the whole family came in for an immense amount of vituperation.

Then Pip received a thrashing, in spite of Judy's persistent avowal that it was all her fault, and Pip hadn't done anything. She remembered wondering whether she would be treated as summarily as Pip, so angry was her father's face as he pushed the boy aside and stood looking at her, riding-whip in hand.

But he flung it down and laid a heavy hand on her shrinking shoulder.

"Next Monday," he said slowly—"next Monday morning you will go to boarding-school. Esther, kindly see that her clothes are ready for boarding-school—next Monday morning."

From *Seven Little Australians* (1894)

The Lucky Baby

A. P. HERBERT

My father went off with a gypsy,
   Had seventeen children and died;
My mother was touchy and tipsy,
   But I was her joy and her pride;
And many's the penny I've brought her
   Down Ascot and Newmarket way—
She'd hold up her seventeenth daughter
   To the lords and the ladies, and say:

"Spare a copper for the Lucky Baby!
   Lucky Elizabeth Maud!
      She'll bring you such luck, sir,
      You never have struck, sir,
Health, winners, and travel abroad.
Hold up, Lucky Liz, show his lordship your phiz—
   How's that for a fortunate face?
      The last and the luckiest,
      Prettiest, pluckiest,
Lucky Elizabeth Grace!"

My face was my fortune, she told me.
    And that's all the fortune I've seen;
I loved a young man, but he sold me,
    And I married the next at eighteen.
Well, one thing leads on to another,
    My husband has left me again,
And now I'm a happy young mother,
    At Epsom you'll hear me complain:

"Throw out your coppers for the Lucky Baby,
Lucky Elizabeth Loo!
You couldn't refuse her,
You won't have a loser—
Milord, you've a lucky face, too.
Hold up, Lucky Rose, show the lady your nose:
Now ain't that a fortunate eye?
The first one is lucky,
They say, don't they, ducky?
God bless you, milady—goodbye!"

"Spare a copper for the Lucky Baby,
And blessings shall be your reward.
She's a regular fairy,
Brought luck to Queen Mary,
Health and wealth to the motherless lord.
Who sent the kind stork to the Duchess of York,
And cured our dear Prince of his pain?
Well, you ask the Prince
If he's had the croup since
He was good to Elizabeth Jane!"

From *Plain Jane* (1927)

Being Wanted

E. NESBIT

The five children, seeking some novel occupation, go digging in nearby sandpits—and uncover a sand-fairy, or Psammead. As a result, whatever they wish comes true—and although this may sound an excellent situation in which to find yourself, it can have drawbacks.

The morning after the children had been the possessors of boundless wealth, and had been unable to buy anything really useful or enjoyable with it, except two pairs of cotton gloves, twelve penny buns, an imitation crocodile-skin purse, and a ride in a pony-cart, they awoke without any of the enthusiastic happiness which they had felt on the previous day when they remembered how they had had the luck to find a Psammead, or Sand-fairy; and to receive its promise to grant them a new wish every day. For now they had had two wishes, Beauty and Wealth, and neither had exactly made them happy. But the happening of strange things, even if they are not completely pleasant things, is more amusing than those times when nothing happens but meals, and they are not always completely pleasant, especially on the days when it is cold mutton or hash.

There was no chance of talking things over before breakfast, because everyone overslept itself, as it happened, and it needed a vigorous and determined struggle to get dressed so as to be only ten minutes late for breakfast. During this meal some efforts were made to deal with the question of the Psammead in an impartial spirit, but it is very difficult to discuss anything thoroughly and at the same time to attend faithfully to your baby brother's breakfast needs. The Baby was particularly lively that morning. He not only wriggled his body through the bar of his high chair, and hung by his head, choking and purple, but he collared a tablespoon with desperate suddenness, hit Cyril heavily on the head with it, and then cried because it was taken away from him. He put his fat fist in his bread-and-milk, and demanded "nam", which was only allowed for tea. He sang, he put his feet on the table—he clamoured to "go walky". The conversation was something like this:

"Look here—about that Sand-fairy—Look out!—he'll have the milk over."

Milk removed to a safe distance.

"Yes—about that Fairy—No, Lamb dear, give Panther the narky poon."

Then Cyril tried. "Nothing we've had yet has turned out— He nearly had the mustard that time!"

"I wonder whether we'd better wish—Hullo!—you've done it now, my boy!" And, in a flash of glass and pink baby-paws, the bowl of golden carp in the middle of the table rolled on its side, and poured a flood of mixed water and goldfish into the Baby's lap and into the laps of the others.

Everyone was almost as much upset as the goldfish; the Lamb only remaining calm. When the pool on the floor had been mopped up, and the leaping, gasping goldfish had been collected and put back in the water, the Baby was taken away to be entirely redressed by Martha, and most of the others had to change completely. The pinafores and jackets that had been bathed in goldfish-and-water were hung out to dry, and then it turned out that Jane must either mend the dress she had torn the day before or appear all day in her best petti-coat. It was white and soft and frilly, and trimmed with lace, and very, very pretty, quite as pretty as a frock, if not more so. Only it was *not* a frock, and Martha's word was law. She wouldn't let Jane wear her best frock, and she refused to listen for a moment to Robert's suggestion that Jane should wear her best petticoat and call it a dress.

"It's not respectable," she said. And when people say that, it's no use anyone's saying anything. You will find this out for yourselves some day.

So there was nothing for it but for Jane to mend her frock. The hole had been torn the day before when she happened to tumble down in the High Street of Rochester, just where a water-cart had passed on its silvery way. She had grazed her knee, and her stocking was much more than grazed, and her dress was cut by the same stone which had attended to the knee and the stocking. Of course the others were not such sneaks as to abandon a comrade in misfortune, so they all sat on the grass-plot round the sundial, and Jane darned away for dear life. The Lamb was still in the hands of Martha having its clothes changed, so conversation was possible.

Anthea and Robert timidly tried to conceal their inmost thought, which was that the Psammead was not to be trusted; but Cyril said:

"Speak out—say what you've got to say—I hate hinting, and 'don't know', and sneakish ways like that."

So then Robert said, as in honour bound: "Sneak yourself —Anthea and me weren't so goldfishy as you two were, so we got changed quicker, and we've had time to think it over, and if you ask me—"

"I didn't ask you," said Jane, biting off a needleful of thread as she had always been strictly forbidden to do.

"I don't care who asks or who doesn't," said Robert, "but Anthea and I think the Sammyadd is a spiteful brute. If it can give us our wishes I suppose it can give itself its own, and I feel almost sure it wishes every time that our wishes shan't do us any good. Let's let the tiresome beast alone, and just go and have a jolly good game of forts, on our own, in the chalk-pit."

(You will remember that the happily situated house where these children were spending their holidays lay between a chalk-quarry and a gravel-pit.)

Cyril and Jane were more hopeful—they generally were.

"I don't think the Sammyadd does it on purpose," Cyril said; "and, after all, it *was* silly to wish for boundless wealth. Fifty pounds in two-shilling pieces would have been much more sensible. And wishing to be beautiful as the day was simply donkeyish. I don't want to be disagreeable, but it *was*. We must try to find a really useful wish, and wish it."

Jane dropped her work and said:

"I think so too, it's too silly to have a chance like this and not use it. I never heard of anyone else outside a book who had such a chance; there must be simply heaps of things we could wish for that wouldn't turn out Dead Sea fish, like these two things have. Do let's think hard, and wish something nice, so that we can have a real jolly day—what there is left of it."

Jane darned away again like mad, for time was indeed getting on, and everyone began to talk at once. If you had been there you could not possibly have made head or tail of the talk, but these children were used to talking "by fours", as soldiers march, and each of them could say what it had to say quite comfortably, and listen to the agreeable sound of its own voice, and at the same time have three-quarters of two sharp ears to spare for listening to what the others said. That is an easy example in multiplication of vulgar fractions, but, as I daresay you can't do even that, I won't ask you to tell me whether $\frac{3}{4} \times 2 = 1\frac{1}{2}$, but I will ask you to believe me that this was the amount of ear each child was able to lend to the others. Lending ears was common in Roman times, as we learn from Shakespeare; but I fear I am getting too instructive.

When the frock was darned, the start for the gravel-pit was delayed by Martha's insisting on everybody's washing its hands—which was nonsense, because nobody had been doing anything at all, except Jane, and how can you get dirty doing nothing? That is a difficult question, and I cannot answer it on paper. In real life I could very soon show you—or you me, which is much more likely.

During the conversation in which the six ears were lent (there were four children, so *that* sum comes right), it had been decided that fifty pounds in two-shilling pieces was the right wish to have. And the lucky children, who could have anything in the wide world by just wishing for it, hurriedly started for the gravel-pit to express their wishes to the Psammead. Martha caught them at the gate, and insisted on their taking the Baby with them.

"Not want him indeed! Why, everybody 'ud want him, a duck! with all their hearts they would; and you know you promised your ma to take him out every blessed day," said Martha.

"I know we did," said Robert in gloom, "but I wish the Lamb wasn't quite so young and small. It would be much better fun taking him out."

"He'll mend of his youngness with time," said Martha; "and as for his smallness, I don't think you'd fancy carrying of him any more, however big he was. Besides he can walk a bit, bless his precious fat legs, a ducky! He feels the benefit of the new-laid air, so he does, a pet!"

With this and a kiss, she plumped the Lamb into Anthea's arms, and went back to make new pinafores on the sewing-machine. She was a rapid performer on this instrument.

The Lamb laughed with pleasure, and said, "Walky wif Panty," and rode on Robert's back with yells of joy, and tried to feed Jane with stones, and altogether made himself so agreeable that nobody could long be sorry that he was of the party.

The enthusiastic Jane even suggested that they should devote a week's wishes to assuring the Baby's future, by asking such gifts for him as the good fairies give to Infant Princes in proper fairy-tales, but Anthea soberly reminded her that as the Sand-fairy's wishes only lasted till sunset they could not ensure any benefit to the Baby's later years; and Jane owned that it would be better to wish for fifty pounds in two-shilling pieces, and buy the Lamb a three-pound-fifteen rocking-horse, like those in the Army and Navy Stores list, with part of the money.

It was settled that, as soon as they had wished for the money and got it, they would get Mr Crispin to drive them into Rochester again, taking Martha with them, if they could not get out of taking her. And they would make a list of the things they really wanted before they started. Full of high hopes and excellent resolutions, they went round the safe slow cart-road to the gravel-pits, and as they went in between the mounds of gravel a sudden thought came to them, and would have turned their ruddy cheeks pale if they had been children in a book. Being real live children, it only made them stop and look at each other with rather blank and silly expressions. For now they remembered that yesterday, when they had asked the Psammead for boundless wealth, and it was getting ready to fill the quarry with the minted gold of bright guineas—millions of them—it had told the children to run along outside the quarry for fear they should be buried alive in the heavy splendid treasure. And they had run. And so it happened that they had not had time to mark the spot where the Psammead was, with a ring of stones, as before. And it was this thought that put such silly expressions on their faces.

"Never mind," said the hopeful Jane, "we'll soon find him."

But this, though easily said, was hard in the doing. They looked and they looked, and though they found their seaside spades, nowhere could they find the Sand-fairy.

At last they had to sit down and rest—not at all because they were weary or disheartened, of course, but because the Lamb insisted on being put down, and you cannot look very carefully after anything you may have happened to lose in the sand if you have an active baby to look after at the same time. Get someone to drop your best knife in the sand next time you go to the seaside, and then take your baby brother with you when you go to look for it, and you will see that I am right.

The Lamb, as Martha had said, was feeling the benefit of the country air, and he was as frisky as a sand-hopper. The elder ones longed to go on talking about the new wishes they would have when (or if) they found the Psammead again. But the Lamb wished to enjoy himself.

He watched his opportunity and threw a handful of sand into Anthea's face, and then suddenly burrowed his own head in the sand and waved his fat legs in the air. Then of course the sand got into his eyes, as it had into Anthea's, and he howled.

The thoughtful Robert had brought one solid brown bottle of ginger-beer with him, relying on a thirst that had never yet failed him. This had to be uncorked hurriedly—it was the only wet thing within reach, and it was necessary to wash the sand out of the Lamb's eyes somehow. Of course the ginger hurt horribly, and he howled more than ever. And, amid his anguish of kicking, the bottle was upset and the beautiful ginger-beer frothed out into the sand and was lost for ever.

It was then that Robert, usually a very patient brother, so far forgot himself as to say:

"Anybody would want him, indeed! Only they don't; Martha doesn't, not really, or she'd jolly well keep him with her. He's a little nuisance, that's what he is. It's too bad. I only wish everybody *did* want him with all their hearts; we might get some peace in our lives."

The Lamb stopped howling now, because Jane had suddenly remembered that there is only one safe way of taking things out of little children's eyes, and that is with your own soft wet tongue. It is quite easy if you love the Baby as much as you ought to.

Then there was a little silence. Robert was not proud of himself for having been so cross, and the others were not proud of him either. You often notice that sort of silence when someone has said something it ought not to—and everyone else holds its tongue and waits for the one who oughtn't to have said it is sorry.

The silence was broken by a sigh—a breath suddenly let out. The children's heads turned as if there had been a string tied to each nose, and someone had pulled all the strings at once.

And everyone saw the Sand-fairy sitting quite close to them, with the expression which it used as a smile on its hairy face.

"Good-morning," it said; "I did that quite easily! Every-one wants him now."

"It doesn't matter," said Robert sulkily, because he knew he had been behaving rather like a pig. "No matter who wants him—there's no one here to—anyhow."

"Ingratitude," said the Psammead, "is a dreadful vice."

"We're not ungrateful," Jane made haste to say, "but we didn't *really* want that wish. Robert only just said it. Can't you take it back and give us a new one?"

"No—I can't," the Sand-fairy said shortly: "chopping and changing—it's not business. You ought to be careful what you *do* wish. There was a little boy once, he'd wished for a Plesiosaurus instead of an Ichthyosaurus, because he was too lazy to remember the easy names of everyday things, and his father had been very vexed with him, and had made him go to bed before tea-time, and wouldn't let him go out in the nice flint boat along with the other children—it was the annual school-treat next day—and he came and flung himself down near me on the morning of the treat, and he kicked his little prehistoric legs about and said he wished he was dead. And of course then he was."

"How awful!" said the children all together.

"Only till sunset, of course," the Psammead said; "still it was quite enough for his father and mother. And he caught it when he woke up—I can tell you. He didn't turn to stone—I forget why—but there must have been some reason. They didn't know being dead is only being asleep, and you're bound to wake up somewhere or other, either where you go to sleep or in some better place. You may be sure he caught it, giving them such a turn. Why, he wasn't allowed to taste Megatherium for a month after that. Nothing but oysters and periwinkles, and common things like that."

All the children were quite crushed by this terrible tale. They looked at the Psammead in horror. Suddenly the Lamb perceived that something brown and furry was near him.

"Poof, poof, poofy," he said, and made a grab.

"It's not a pussy," Anthea was beginning, when the Sand-fairy leaped back.

"Oh, my left whisker!" it said; "don't let him touch me. He's wet."

Its fur stood on end with horror—and indeed a good deal of the ginger-beer had been spilt on the blue smock of the Lamb.

The Psammead dug with its hands and feet, and vanished in an instant and a whirl of sand.

The children marked the spot with a ring of stones.

"We may as well get along home," said Robert. "I'll say I'm sorry; but anyway if it's no good it's no harm, and we know where the sandy thing is for to-morrow."

The others were noble. No one reproached Robert at all. Cyril picked up the Lamb, who was now quite himself again, and off they went by the safe cart-road.

The cart-road from the gravel-pits joins the road almost directly.

At the gate into the road the party stopped to shift the Lamb from Cyril's back to Robert's. And as they paused a very smart open carriage came in sight, with a coachman and a groom on the box, and inside the carriage a lady—very grand indeed, with a dress all white lace and red ribbons and a parasol all red and white—and a white fluffy dog on her lap with a red ribbon round its neck. She looked at the children, and particularly at the Baby, and she smiled at him. The children were used to this, for the Lamb was, as all the servants said, a "very taking child". So they waved their hands politely to the lady and expected her to drive on. But she did not. Instead she made the coachman stop. And she beckoned to Cyril, and when he went up to the carriage she said:

"What a dear darling duck of a baby! Oh, I *should* so like to adopt it! Do you think its mother would mind?"

"She'd mind very much indeed," said Anthea shortly.

"Oh, but I should bring it up in luxury, you know. I am Lady Chittenden. You must have seen my photograph in the illustrated papers. They call me a beauty, you know, but of course that's all nonsense. Anyway—"

She opened the carriage door and jumped out. She had the wonderfullest red high-heeled shoes with silver buckles. "Let me hold him a minute," she said. And she took the Lamb and held him very awkwardly, as if she was not used to babies.

Then suddenly she jumped into the carriage with the Lamb in her arms and slammed the door and said, "Drive on!"

The Lamb roared, the little white dog barked, and the coachman hesitated.

"Drive on, I tell you!" cried the lady; and the coachman did, for, as he said afterwards, it was as much as his place was worth not to.

The four children looked at each other, and then with one accord they rushed after the carriage and held on behind. Down the dusty road went the smart carriage, and after it, at double-quick time, ran the twinkling legs of the Lamb's brothers and sisters.

The Lamb howled louder and louder, but presently his howls changed by slow degree to hiccupy gurgles, and then all was still and they knew he had gone to sleep.

The carriage went on, and the eight feet that twinkled through the dust were growing quite stiff and tired before the carriage stopped at the lodge of a grand park. The children crouched down behind the carriage, and the lady got out. She

looked at the Baby as it lay on the carriage seat, and hesitated.

"The darling—I won't disturb it," she said, and went into
the lodge to talk to the woman there about a setting of Buff
Orpington eggs that had not turned out well.

The coachman and footman sprang from the box and bent
over the sleeping Lamb.

"Fine boy—wish he was mine," said the coachman.

"He wouldn't favour *you* much," said the groom sourly;
"too 'andsome."

The coachman pretended not to hear. He said:

"Wonder at her now—I do really! Hates kids. Got none of
her own, and can't abide other folkses'."

The children, crouching in the white dust under the carriage, exchanged uncomfortable glances.

"Tell you what," the coachman went on firmly, "blowed
if I don't hide the little nipper in the hedge and tell her his
brothers took 'im! Then I'll come back for him afterwards."

"No, you don't," said the footman. "I've took to that kid
so as never was. If anyone's to have him, it's me—so there!"

"Stow your gab!" the coachman rejoined. "You don't want
no kids, and, if you did, one kid's the same as another to you.
But I'm a married man and a judge of breed. I knows a first-
rate yearling when I sees him. I'm a-goin' to 'ave him, an'
least said soonest mended."

"I should 'a' thought," said the footman sneeringly, "you'd
a'most enough. What with Alfred, an' Albert, an' Louise, an'
Victor Stanley, and Helena Beatrice, and another—"

The coachman hit the footman in the chin—the footman
hit the coachman in the waistcoat—the next minute the two
were fighting here and there, in and out, up and down, and
all over everywhere, and the little dog jumped on the box of
the carriage and began barking like mad.

Cyril, still crouching in the dust, waddled on bent legs to the side of the carriage farthest from the battlefield. He unfastened the door of the carriage—the two men were far too much occupied with their quarrel to notice anything—took the Lamb in his arms, and, still stooping, carried the sleeping baby a dozen yards along the road to where a stile led into a wood. The others followed, and there among the hazels and young oaks and sweet chestnuts, covered by high strong-scented bracken, they all lay hidden till the angry voices of the men were hushed at the angry voice of the red-and-white lady, and, after a long and anxious search, the carriage at last drove away.

"My only hat!" said Cyril, drawing a deep breath as the sound of wheels at last died away. "Everyone *does* want him now—and no mistake! That Sammeadd has done us again! Tricky brute! For any sake, let's get the kid safe home."

So they peeped out, and finding on the right hand only lonely white road, and nothing but lonely white road on the left, they took courage, and the road, Anthea carrying the sleeping Lamb.

Adventures dogged their footsteps. A boy with a bundle of faggots on his back dropped his bundle by the roadside and asked to look at the Baby, and then offered to carry him; but Anthea was not to be caught that way twice. They all walked on, but the boy followed, and Cyril and Robert couldn't make him go away till they had more than once invited him to smell their fists. Afterwards a little girl in a blue-and-white checked pinafore actually followed them for a quarter of a mile crying for "the precious Baby", and then she was only got rid of by threats of tying her to a tree in the wood with all their pocket-handkerchiefs. "So that the bears can come and eat you as soon as it gets dark," said Cyril severely. Then she went off crying. It presently seemed wise, to the brothers and

sisters of the Baby, who was wanted by everyone, to hide in
the hedge whenever they saw anyone coming, and thus they
managed to prevent the Lamb from arousing the inconvenient affection of a milkman, a stone-breaker, and a man
who drove a cart with a paraffin barrel at the back of it. They
were nearly home when the worst thing of all happened.
Turning a corner suddenly they came upon two vans, a tent,
and a company of gipsies encamped by the side of the road.
The vans were hung all round with wicker chairs and cradles,
and flower-stands and feather brushes. A lot of ragged children were industriously making dust-pies in the road, two men

lay on the grass smoking, and three women were doing the family washing in an old red watering-can with the top broken off.

In a moment all the gipsies, men, women, and children, surrounded Anthea and the Baby.

"Let *me* hold him, little lady," said one of the gipsy women, who had a mahogany-coloured face and dust-coloured hair; "I won't hurt a hair of his head, the little picture!"

"I'd rather not," said Anthea.

"Let me have him," said the other woman, whose face was also of the hue of mahogany, and her hair jet-black, in greasy curls. "I've nineteen of my own, so I have."

"No," said Anthea bravely, but her heart beat so that it nearly choked her.

Then one of the men pushed forward.

"Swelp me if it ain't!" he cried, "my own long-lost cheild! Have he a strawberry mark on his left ear? No? Then he's my own babby, stolen from me in hinnocent hinfancy. 'And 'im over—and we'll not 'ave the law on yer this time."

He snatched the Baby from Anthea, who turned scarlet and burst into tears of pure rage.

The others were standing quite still; this was much the most terrible thing that had ever happened to them. Even being taken up by the police in Rochester was nothing to this. Cyril was quite white, and his hands trembled a little, but he made a sign to the others to shut up. He was silent a minute, thinking hard. Then he said:

"We don't want to keep him if he's yours. But you see he's used to us. You shall have him if you want him."

"No, no!" cried Anthea—and Cyril glared at her.

"Of course we want him," said the women, trying to get the Baby out of the man's arms. The Lamb howled loudly.

"Oh, he's hurt!" shrieked Anthea; and Cyril, in a savage undertone, bade her "Stow it!"

"You trust to me," he whispered. "Look here," he went on, "he's awfully tiresome with people he doesn't know very well. Suppose we stay here a bit till he gets used to you, and then when it's bedtime I give you my word of honour we'll go away and let you keep him if you want to. And then when we're gone you can decide which of you is to have him, as you all want him so much."

"That's fair enough," said the man who was holding the Baby, trying to loosen the red neckerchief which the Lamb had caught hold of and drawn round his mahogany throat so tight that he could hardly breathe. The gipsies whispered together, and Cyril took the chance to whisper too. He said, "Sunset! we'll get away then."

And then his brothers and sisters were filled with wonder and admiration at his having been so clever as to remember this.

"Oh, do let him come to us!" said Jane. "See we'll sit down here and take care of him for you till he gets used to you."

"What about dinner?" said Robert suddenly. The others

looked at him with scorn. "Fancy bothering about your beastly dinner when your br—I mean when the Baby"—Jane whispered hotly. Robert carefully winked at her and went on:

"You won't mind my just running home to get our dinner?" he said to the gipsy; "I can bring it out here in a basket."

His brothers and sisters felt themselves very noble, and despised him. They did not know his thoughtful secret intention. But the gipsies did in a minute.

"Oh yes!" they said; "and then fetch the police with a pack of lies about it being your baby instead of ours! D'jever catch a weasel asleep?" they asked.

"If you're hungry you can pick a bit along of us," said the light-haired gipsy woman, not unkindly. "Here, Levi, that blessed kid'll howl all his buttons off. Give him to the little lady, and let's see if they can't get him used to us a bit."

So the Lamb was handed back; but the gipsies crowded so closely that he could not possibly stop howling. Then the man with the red handkerchief said:

"Here, Pharaoh, make up the fire; and you girls see to the pot. Give the kid a chanst." So the gipsies, very much against their will, went off to their work, and the children and the Lamb were left sitting on the grass.

"He'll be all right at sunset," Jane whispered. "But, oh, it is awful! Suppose they are frightfully angry when they come to their senses! They might beat us, or leave us tied to trees, or something."

"No, they won't," Anthea said. ("Oh, my Lamb, don't cry any more, it's all right, Panty's got oo, duckie!") "They aren't unkind people, or they wouldn't be going to give us any dinner."

"Dinner?" said Robert. "I won't touch their nasty dinner.

It would choke me!"

The others thought so too then. But when the dinner was ready—it turned out to be supper, and happened between four and five—they were all glad enough to take what they could get. It was boiled rabbit, with onions, and some bird rather like a chicken, but stringier about its legs and with a stronger taste. The Lamb had bread soaked in hot water and brown sugar sprinkled on the top. He liked this very much, and consented to let the two gipsy women feed him with it, as he sat on Anthea's lap. All that long hot afternoon Robert and Cyril and Anthea and Jane had to keep the Lamb amused and happy, while the gipsies looked eagerly on. By the time the shadows grew long and black across the meadows he had really "taken to" the woman with the light hair, and even consented to kiss his hand to the children, and to stand up and bow, with his hand on his chest—"like a gentleman"—to the two men. The whole gipsy camp was in raptures with him, and his brothers and sisters could not help taking some pleasure in showing off his accomplishments to an audience so interested and enthusiastic. But they longed for sunset.

"We're getting into the habit of longing for sunset," Cyril whispered. "How I do wish we could wish something really sensible, that would be of some use, so that we should be quite sorry when sunset came."

The shadows got longer and longer, and at last there were no separate shadows any more, but one soft glowing shadow over everything; for the sun was out of sight—behind the hill —but he had not really set yet. The people who make the laws about lighting bicycle lamps are the people who decide when the sun sets; he has to do it, too, to the minute, or they would know the reason why!

But the gipsies were getting impatient.

"Now, young uns," the red-handkerchief man said, "it's time you were laying of your heads on your pillowses—so it is! The kid's all right and friendly with us now—so you just hand him over and sling that hook o' yours like you said."

The women and children came crowding round the Lamb, arms were held out, fingers snapped invitingly, friendly faces beaming with admiring smiles; but all failed to tempt the loyal Lamb. He clung with arms and legs to Jane, who happened to be holding him, and uttered the gloomiest roar of the whole day.

"It's no good," the woman said, "hand the little poppet over, miss. We'll soon quiet him."

And still the sun would not set.

"Tell her about how to put him to bed," whispered Cyril; "anything to gain time—and be ready to bolt when the sun really does make up its silly old mind to set."

"Yes, I'll hand him over in just one minute," Anthea began, talking very fast—"but do let me just tell you he has a warm bath every night and cold in the morning, and he has a crockery rabbit to go into the warm bath with him, and little Samuel saying his prayers in white china on a red cushion for the cold bath; and if you let the soap get into his eyes, the Lamb—"

"Lamb kyes," said he—he had stopped roaring to listen.

The woman laughed. "As if I hadn't never bath'd a babby!" she said. "Come—give us hold of him. Come to 'Melia, my precious."

"G'way, ugsie!" replied the Lamb at once.

"Yes, but," Anthea went on, "about his meals; you really *must* let me tell you he has an apple or a banana every morning, and bread-and-milk for breakfast, and an egg for his tea sometimes, and—"

"I've brought up ten," said the black-ringleted woman,

"besides the others. Come, miss, 'and 'im over—I can't bear it no longer. I just must give him a hug."

"We ain't settled yet whose he's to be, Esther," said one of the men.

"It won't be you, Esther, with seven of 'em at your tail a'ready."

"I ain't so sure of that," said Esther's husband.

"And ain't I nobody, to have a say neither?" said the husband of 'Melia.

Zillah, the girl, said, "An' me? I'm a single girl—and no one but 'im to look after—I ought to have him."

"Hold yer tongue!"

"Shut your mouth!"

"Don't you show me no more of your imperence!"

Everyone was getting very angry. The dark gipsy faces were frowning and anxious-looking. Suddenly a change swept over them, as if some invisible sponge had wiped away these cross and anxious expressions, and left only a blank.

The children saw that the sun really *had* set. But they were afraid to move. And the gipsies were feeling so muddled, because of the invisible sponge that had washed all the feelings of the last few hours out of their hearts, that they could not say a word.

The children hardly dared to breathe. Suppose the gipsies, when they recovered speech, should be furious to think how silly they had been all day?

It was an awkward moment. Suddenly Anthea, greatly daring, held out the Lamb to the red-handkerchief man.

"Here he is!" she said.

The man drew back. "I shouldn't like to deprive you, miss," he said hoarsely.

"Anyone who likes to have my share of him," said the other man.

"After all, I've got enough of my own," said Esther.

"He's a nice little chap, though," said Amelia. She was the only one who now looked affectionately at the whimpering Lamb.

Zillah said, "If I don't think I must have had a touch of the sun. *I* don't want him."

"Then shall we take him away?" said Anthea.

"Well, suppose you do," said Pharaoh heartily, "and we'll say no more about it!"

And with great haste all the gipsies began to be busy about their tents for the night. All but Amelia. She went with the children as far as the bend in the road—and there she said:

"Let me give him a kiss, miss—I don't know what made us go for to behave so silly. Us gipsies don't steal babies, whatever they may tell you when you're naughty. We've enough of our own, mostly. But I've lost all mine."

She leaned towards the Lamb; and he, looking in her eyes, unexpectedly put up a grubby soft paw and stroked her face.

"Poor, poor!" said the Lamb. And he let the gipsy woman kiss him, and, what is more, he kissed her brown cheek in return—a very nice kiss, as all his kisses are, and not a wet one like some babies give. The gipsy woman moved her finger about on his forehead, as if she had been writing something there, and the same with his chest and his hands and his feet; then she said:

"May he be brave, and have the strong head to think with, and the strong heart to love with, and the strong hands to work with, and the strong feet to travel with, and always come safe home to his own." Then she said something in a strange language no one could understand, and suddenly added:

"Well, I must be saying 'so long'—and glad to have made

your acquaintance." And she turned and went back to her home—the tent by the grassy roadside.

The children looked after her till she was out of sight. Then Robert said, "How silly of her! Even sunset didn't put *her* right. What rot she talked!"

"Well," said Cyril, "if you ask me, I think it was rather decent of her—"

"Decent?" said Anthea; "it was very nice indeed of her. I think she's a dear."

"She's just too frightfully nice for anything," said Jane.

And they went home—very late for tea and unspeakably late for dinner. Martha scolded, of course. But the Lamb was safe.

"I say—it turned out we wanted the Lamb as much as anyone," said Robert, later.

"Of course."

"But do you feel different about it now the sun's set?"

"*No*," said all the others together.

"Then it's lasted over sunset with us."

"No, it hasn't," Cyril explained. "The wish didn't do anything to *us*. We always wanted him with all our hearts when we were our proper selves, only we were all pigs this morning; especially you, Robert." Robert bore this much with a strange calm.

"I certainly *thought* I didn't want him this morning," said he. "Perhaps I was a pig. But everything looked so different when we thought we were going to lose him."

From *Five Children and It* (1902)

The Baby Show

EVE GARNETT

"I can't understand it!" said Mrs. Ruggles to her friend Mrs. Mullet, as they stood blocking the pavement outside the Home and Continental Stores with their respective prams during a lull in the family shopping one afternoon. "Ten months old on Saturday and not a tooth showing! If it had been Kate now, what were the skinniest infant as ever you saw—mere rasher of wind she were—but a fine big baby like William! And if it isn't just our luck too! You see, Mrs. Mullet, it's like this. Here's my husband been objecting all these years to Baby Shows—both feet down you might say— and us with fine twins too! Obstinate? That's not the word; then one day, home he comes, full of this Feat what's holding in the old Priory Grounds next week. He says to me, 'Rosie,' he says, 'there's a Baby Show connected, what about our William?' 'What about him?' I says, trying not to sound surprised, though you might have knocked me down with a feather! 'William's finer nor any baby I've seen about,' he goes on, 'bigger'n Albert Bird's grandson now, wouldn't you say—they're showing him?' 'Why William u'd make three of

214

him, the miserable little worm,' I says—'bit slow with his teeth perhaps, but he'll have plenty afore this show comes along.' 'It's only six weeks,' says Jo, 'can't we do nothing to hurry 'em on—dog-biscuits or summat?' 'Dog-biscuits!' I cried, 'why whatever are you thinking of, Jo Ruggles!' Well, I thought it were only a father's anxiety for the prize, Mrs. Mullet, and I were so pleased at the idea of showing a baby at last, and so afraid Jo might change his mind, that I says no more. However, after a bit I began to get suspicious-like. Jo kept on worriting about William all day long; if it weren't his teeth it were his weight or his hair or how long he could sit up. Then one evening, coming back from the allotment we meets Albert Bird. 'How's William?' he says. 'Fine, thanks,' I replies. 'Cut any teeth yet?' he asks. 'Half a dozen any day now,' I says, and whatever's an old man like you so interested for, I thinks to myself. 'My George's baby's got five,' he says, and with that he slaps Jo on the back and roars with laughter! Then I know my suspicions hadn't been for nothing; there was something up! 'And I'm not going home till I knows what!' I says. Well, they was both hungry and wanted their suppers, so I soon had it out of them. And would you believe it, Mrs. Mullet, it was betting they'd been —my Jo, what never even backs a football, much less a horse, betting on a baby! A whole half-crown on William against the baby Bird! It gave me quite a turn; almost indecent it seemed, but I've come round since; the deed's done, and better babies than horses, I says to myself (though I hope it won't lead to them), and after all I've always wanted to show a baby, there's big money in prizes, and I wants that half-crown back! But you see now what I mean, Mrs. Mullet, when I says luck's against us. Here's William, ten months old on Saturday, the show's next Wednesday, and not a tooth he's got!"

Mrs. Mullet was very sympathetic. Although she was not certain whether she altogether "held" with Baby Shows—anyway, her Muriel was nearly three and past the age limit—she understood the value of half a crown.

"You've tried the Welfare, I suppose?" she said.

Mrs. Ruggles nodded. "The doctor says 'don't worry; his gums is hard as hard; he'll cut one any day,' but she don't know which day no more than you or I, Mrs. Mullet!"—Rusks? A wooden ring? A chicken bone to chew? Mrs. Ruggles had tried them all.

"It will have to be the dog-biscuits," laughed Mrs. Mullet, as she prepared to move on.

"I'll not poison my William for all the Baby Shows in England!" declared Mrs. Ruggles. "It's Nature or Nothing for me; well, see you at the show, Mrs. Mullet, and wish us luck!"

"That I will, Mrs. Ruggles, you can count on me; I can't abide that George Bird family, anyway," she added as they parted.

Wednesday dawned bright and sunny—a perfect day for a Fête, but it could not cheer the drooping spirits of the Ruggles family. William was toothless! He had been what Mrs. Ruggles called "fretty" half the night, a state that would have almost certainly heralded the arrival of a tooth in any of her other children. He now lay peacefully sleeping on two cushions in a corner of the kitchen; his brothers and sisters crowded round him as if by looking they could in some way induce a tooth to show itself.

"Keep away from him, do," said Mrs. Ruggles sharply. She had had a very disturbed night, and the prospect of a day's ironing compressed into a hot morning was not encouraging. "No you can't all come to the Fête," she cried presently in answer to Lily Rose's inquiry. "It'll be sixpence

each for your father and me, threepence for Peg, and threepence each for all of you after five—that's half a crown. Lily
Rose and Kate can come, the rest of you'll have to stay at
home."

"Oh, let 'em all come," said Mr. Ruggles, getting up from
his breakfast and throwing half a crown on the table. Mr.
Ruggles looked despondent; had he been allowed his way
about the dog-biscuits, all, he was sure, would now be well
but he knew it was more than his life was worth to say so at
the moment.

"Half-crowns seems nothing to you, these days!" said his
wife sarcastically, and Mr. Ruggles put on his cap, hunched
up his shoulders and departed to his work, looking what he
felt, a very ill-used man.

No sooner had the elder children gone off to school, than
William became "fretty" again. Nothing seemed to soothe
him. "Wear himself out, he will, crying like this," said Mrs.
Ruggles distractedly. To assist matters, Peg was more than
usually full of spirits, and in her most adventurous mood, and
by the time Mrs. Ruggles had twice placed a knife and pair
of scissors beyond reach, and rescued her daughter from the
flour bin and blacklead box, she had decided she would support no Government in future that did not promise immedi-
ate erection of Nursery Schools to accommodate under
school-age offspring, and relieve harassed mothers.

But when she set forth at two o'clock, all these worries had
vanished; Peg was subdued and tidy in a clean cotton frock,
and William, in his best yellow woollies, was all gurgles and
smiles again. Teeth or no teeth, thought Mrs. Ruggles, he
certainly was a remarkably fine baby, and she was much
elated by some flattering remarks she heard "passed" by the
crowd outside the Manor gates, and the nervous glances cast
at her perambulator by some of the other mothers.

The Fête, which was being held in the grounds of Otwell Priory, an old sixteenth-century house on the outskirts of the town, was in full swing when they arrived. Two marquees had been erected on the lawns, one reserved for tea, the other for the babies, while the less refined part of the entertainment, merry-go-rounds, Hooplas, coconut shies, etc., was relegated to a field behind the house. Even so, the noise they made was deafening, and Mrs. Ruggles was concerned lest William, who had fallen asleep, should be awakened unnecessarily. There were numerous stalls dotted about, and still more numerous ladies who, with fixed smiles, approached Mrs. Ruggles, begging her to guess the weight of a cake, name a doll, or forecast the number of fruits (species unknown) bottled in a jar. But Mrs. Ruggles had not come to waste money; she had come to make it and retrieve her husband's half-crown, and she replied firmly "not to-day, thank you," and succeeded in reaching the baby-tent with her purse unopened.

Heavens! how many babies! Babies in every direction! Fat and thin, dark and fair, plain and beautiful, crying and placid! "And they say the birthrate's going down!" said Mrs. Ruggles to herself. "Well, it don't look like it to me—not in Otwell, anyway."

Each baby seemed to be accompanied by at least three adults, there was a fair sprinkling of small children, and the heat in the tent was stifling. William had awakened and was gazing about him in placid good humour; long might it last, thought Mrs. Ruggles—but really, this heat! Phew!

Presently a bell was rung and a man's voice, speaking through a megaphone, demanded that everyone but the children's mothers please leave the tent, and as soon as a very large lady who loudly and indignantly demanded whether aunties what had brought a motherless baby up from the mouth, were to be excluded, had been reassured, the crowd of onlookers drifted away and the real business of the afternoon began. The babies were divided into two classes: those over six months but under a year old, and those of one year and over but under two years old. Two prizes were offered in each class, and a grand silver-gilt challenge cup for the best baby in the show.

"Look well on my dresser, that would," thought Mrs. Ruggles, as she seated herself in the queue of waiting mothers and began to take stock of the other competitors. They seemed fine specimens on the whole, and she was sorry to see that the under one year section appeared to be by far the most popular. Farther up in the queue she spied young Mrs. George Bird. Heavens! if that woman hadn't gone and dressed her poor child in bright pink woollies the colour of Otwell Rock . . . still, when you remembered what she could put on her own back, perhaps it wasn't so surprising . . .

At the end of the tent a space had been screened off by curtains, and presently the judges, a doctor, and two nurses in uniform arrived to a mixed reception of cheering and wails, and disappeared behind them. Mrs. Ruggles was pleased to see none of them were local people, and that the doctor was well on what she called "the seamy side of forty", for she distrusted young men where babies were concerned. "Shan't be long now!" said the fat auntie who had settled herself on Mrs. Ruggles' left, and almost immediately the Voice, again speaking through the megaphone, announced that the judges were ready—would the competitors please come in one at a time; the results, the Voice added, would be announced outside the tea tent at five-fifteen.

It was over! Mrs. Ruggles, William in her arms and Peg at her side, stood breathing fresh air (and sighs of relief) outside the tent. William had behaved perfectly, smiles and gurgles all the time, even when undressed and weighed, but, whether he had won a prize—! "Ask me something else, Mrs. Mullet!" said Mrs. Ruggles to her friend who was waiting with her Muriel to hear how things had gone. "That doctor was like a sphix, or whatever it is they calls them folks with no expressions. 'Ten months?' he says to me. 'Ten months Saturday,' I says, and hands him the birth certificate. 'No teeth through yet!' he says presently, 'but will have any moment if I'm not mistaken!' and then he writes no end of things in a little book; try as I would, Mrs. Mullet, I couldn't see what! 'Let's have a look at that birth certificate again,' he says, as I were going out, and a look at it he has, and hands it back without a word! No, you can't tell what they thinks, ever, Mrs. Mullet, and the nurses—they're no better— something about a beautiful baby they says, and a seventh child lucky—just talk it is, they learns it them at the Hospital —it don't mean nothing. Well, there's nearly two hours to wait, Mrs. Mullet, afore we knows the worst; how about a nice cup of tea?"

Mrs. Mullet said it was just what she was thinking, and Peg Ruggles, who had been thirsty all the afternoon and said so, at frequent intervals, took Mrs. Mullet's Muriel firmly by one hand, and Mrs. Ruggles by the other, and steered straight for the tea tent!

It was after five o'clock, and a large and impatient crowd was collected in front of the tent. Everyone was full of excited speculation, for in a few minutes the names of the successful babies would be known.

Mrs. Ruggles with William and Peg, and Mrs. Mullet with her Muriel, stood in the front row and were joined at intervals by one after another of the little Ruggles, who had come from school and burrowed their way, impervious to rebukes, through the legs of the onlookers. Mr. Ruggles and old Mr.

Bird had also arrived, much out of breath, and were panting somewhere at the back of the crowd. Everyone began to cheer when punctually at five-fifteen the owner of the Voice, carrying his megaphone, arrived, mounted a chair and announced that, if everyone was listening, he would now with much pleasure call out the names of the successful babies; the prizes, he added, would be presented to the parents by the Mayoress, inside the tent at five-thirty.

The cheering ceased, and a ripple of expectancy passed over the crowd, and then in a silence that was almost frightening, the Voice announced that the Grand Challenge Cup for the best baby in the show had been won by Miss Ada Atkins, aged eighteen months, of Swanwell village; the first prize for babies of one year and over, by Master Freddie Fishwich, aged fourteen months, of Otwell; and the second prize in the same class by Miss Hester (or Esther?) Stribbling, fifteen months, also of Otwell; while in the class for babies under a year old, the first prize was awarded to Master William Ruggles, and the second to Master Albert Bird, both ten months and both of Otwell! The crowd broke into loud cheers, and it was some time before the Voice could be heard trying to continue to speak above the din. "I am asked," it went on, when at last there was a lull in the cheering, "I am asked to say, on behalf of the Committee, that while we are delighted to welcome visitors from outside the Town, and in no way grudge them our prizes, we think it is only fair to let the inhabitants of Otwell know that the Grand Challenge Cup has only narrowly missed being won by the town; in fact, ladies and gentlemen, if the winner in the under one year class, Master William Ruggles, had only been a little hastier in the matter of cutting his teeth, it certainly would have been, and when we have all given three cheers for the winner, Miss Ada Atkins, of Swanwell, I ask you to join in three cheers for Otwell's Best Baby—Master William Ruggles. Now, all together, three cheers for Miss Ada Atkins and her parents, hip, hip—"

"Hurray!" yelled the crowd with great fervour, but the cheers for "Master William Ruggles and his parents" were so deafening that you could hear the echoes almost at One End Street!

"Will the parents please take their babies inside the tent to receive their prizes," said the Voice when at last the applause died away.

"You take him, Jo, I can't!" said Mrs. Ruggles, "I'm all of a tremble!" And Mr. Ruggles, who was all of a tremble himself, having pushed his way through the crowd to the accompaniment of many hearty slaps on the back, proudly held his son while Mrs. Ruggles received a small silver shield and an envelope containing a one-pound note, with many congratulations from the smiling Mayoress.

"Let's get home, quick," said Jo as they emerged from the tent to be greeted by more cheering. Easier said than done; everyone wished to see William, complete strangers wanted to kiss him, gentlemen of the press to take his photograph. Poor Mrs. Ruggles was surrounded, unable to move in any direction, and it was only by the Voice calling through the megaphone that the winner in the raffle for the pair of embroidered bedspreads was being announced at the other end of the grounds, that the crowd could be induced to move away. William now began to cry dismally and his parents seized the opportunity for departure, joined the rest of their family, who in charge of Lily Rose were waiting with the perambulator near the gate, and made for home.

It was not the triumphal procession that one would have expected for Otwell's Best Baby! William's wails increased, and by the time One End Street was reached, he was screaming with a steady persistency that indicated a sleepless night for his relatives. "Tired out he is, poor mite, and wanting his supper, he'll be all right as soon as he gets inside," said his mother. But as soon as the front door was opened William redoubled his yells. "Take him, Lily Rose," commanded Mrs. Ruggles, "while I heats some milk."

Lily Rose obeyed. "Mum!" she cried excitedly a minute later, "come, come quick! He's got it, it's come, William's got a tooth!" Mrs. Ruggles flew to investigate. Too true! and now, alas, too late!

"Would have looked nice there, Jo, the cup," said Mrs. Ruggles sadly, as they passed the dresser on their way to bed that evening. "Perhaps the dog-biscuits would have done it after all!"

But Mr. Ruggles gallantly said no; his Rosie had been right; safer not to go agin' nature, and better William as he were, than a Cup on the dresser and William perhaps dying of dog-biscuits in a Hospital. "Besides," he added, "we can always try again next year."

Rosie looked at him sharply. "We're not having no more babies," she said firmly.

"I only meant," replied Mr. Ruggles, "that as the age limit's two, William 'u'd still be young enough next year."

"I believe," said Mrs. Ruggles, looking hard at him, "I believe, as you wants to make another bet!"

"I've made it!" said Mr. Ruggles. "Albert Bird's took me on again—five bob this time!" he added grinning.

But Mrs. Ruggles' protests were drowned by renewed cries from William.

Another tooth was through!

From *The Family from One End Street* (1937)

The Smell of Privet

BARBARA SLEIGH

A well-loved writer of books for children writes of her own childhood, in Birmingham in the early years of this century. Here she is, acting as admiring follower of her older brother, Linwood . . .

The time the whole family dreaded was the day before my brother went back to school. A pall of gloom descended on the household, which deepened as the evening drew on, and his trunk and tuck-box were locked and corded. But if there were tears in bed at night, there were none at the station next day. In honour bound, this had to be faced dry-eyed and with a stiff upper lip.

My mother and I once went to visit my brother at his prep school, where we stayed for the weekend. Unfortunately we were both a source of embarrassment.

At meal-times I sat next to him among the other boys, in a speechless trance of pride and delight. Unluckily I was at the stage that is entirely without front teeth, and I was quite unable to cope with the crusts of thick bread thought suitable for small boys. Each crust, my brother told me later, curved up from my beaming mouth as I munched the end as best I

could, like the tusk of a wart-hog. However, after some
general laughter, my next-door neighbour, who was a friend
of my brother's, came to my rescue. He cut off all the rest of
my crusts and ate them himself, exchanging them for the
crumb of his. Chivalry could do no more.

Linwood's attendance at the school had been made possible through some manoeuvring on my grandmother's part;
a fact that was freely referred to by the staff. He was told,
for example, that in his position it was up to him to be more
economical with his stationery than the other boys whose
parents paid full fees, and an ingenious series of legends was
invented by a coterie of the crueller wags among his contem-
poraries, of the poverty of the Sleigh family; how my brother
was really an escapee from the local Board School, whose
headmaster might discover him at any minute. But would his
school friends desert him? Never! Whenever this illiterate
monster of a man came to haul him back, they would band
together to hide him. This simply became an excuse to knock
my brother down and sit on him when they had nothing
better to do, while someone, with much snuffling and many
dropped aitches, impersonated the head of the Board School,
to the great entertainment of everyone but my brother.

Unfortunately, when the weekend was over and we were
about to start for the station, the headmaster offered to send
for a cab. My mother's voice was beautiful, but unusually
penetrating, and the whole school on the other side of an
open door heard her reply cheerfully:

"Good gracious, no! We have no money to waste on such
luxuries! If you would be good enough to lend us a walking
stick we can put it through the handle of the suitcase, and
Linwood and I can manage it quite easily between us."
Which is what they did, while I staggered down the drive
behind them with an armful of coats, watched by a row of

delighted faces at the window. My mother was quite oblivious of the humiliation she had caused my scarlet-faced
brother, or of the ammunition she had presented to his perse-
cutors.

Knowing how he dreaded going back to school, I thought
of a plan one holiday to keep him secretly at home. I would
smuggle him into the airing cupboard when it was time for
him to go, where he could hide for the rest of the term. I
was sure I could supply him with enough food without anyone noticing. To humour me he came to investigate the
airing cupboard with a view to thirteen weeks' tenancy, and
though I had to admit, reluctantly, that the quarters really
would be a bit too cramped, for the first time we discovered
the cold-water tank. This was above the shelves of clean
linen, inside a separate cupboard that surprisingly we had
never explored before. When this upper door was opened, it
revealed a narrow shelf in front, on which there was just
room enough to stand, and a large square tank of cold water
behind with a good ten inches between the top and the
ceiling, so that the ball-cock could be investigated to the full.
Surely so much delightful water, there for the playing with,
could be used for something?

"What about a cold bath?" suggested my brother, rather
to my surprise. He was not given to cold baths as a rule. To
my admiration he took off his clothes, climbed up the shelves
of the hot cupboard and squeezed into the tank.

"Are you coming too?" he called down to me as he
splashed about. "It's spiffing!"

I had noticed an odd hissing noise that came out of a
small pipe from time to time and said "No," adding cautiously: "At least, not today." But hating to be outdone I went
on: "I think I'll wash my dolls' clothes up there instead.
They're all pretty dirty."

I went downstairs and fetched some kitchen soap from the store cupboard. It was a whole new bar, about ten inches long, but I wondered if it would be enough for the task I had set myself. Then I collected every stitch of dolls' clothing I could find. It seemed a chance too good to be missed. While with goose-pimpled arms he rubbed himself dry, through chattering teeth my brother explained how much he had enjoyed his bathe. I balanced myself on the little ledge, and using a great deal of soap dabbled my dolls' clothes up and down in the water tank. Not until the bar of soap slipped from my crinkled fingers and sank to the bottom, so that I could not reach it without getting my sleeves wet, did I decide that the clothes were clean enough, and climbed down again.

When my father complained next day of the curious taste of the drinking water, the reason never occurred to us, and when, later still, my mother sent for me and said: "You've been washing your dolls' clothes in the cold tank, haven't you?" I could only put down such perception to some form of second sight. It was not until later that she admitted that the plumber had found the remains of a bar of soap and a doll's sock at the bottom of the tank.

From *The Smell of Privet* (1971)

The Web of the Day

JON AND RUMER GODDEN

Rumer Godden writes for readers of all ages. Here she and her sister, Jon, have combined to tell of their childhood in India, when it was still a part of the British Empire.

In the early morning, mist lay over the river and on the water tanks; it swirled cold on the earth as the sky paled. Then the crows began, glossily black crows with grey necks and wicked, knowing black eyes and beaks; it was their cawing and the whirr of parakeet wings that reached the bedrooms first. Then, from below, the sound of sweeping began: brooms of soft grass in the house, a scratchier sound of twig brooms on the gravel of the path. The sun touched the trees first, until every tip and frond waved in the young light: mangoes, casuarinas, neem trees, acacias, and tall exciting shapes of palms that did not move at all but seemed petrified in colours of greys and greens like palm trees in old prints. The sun spread in a fan of light across the garden, the same shape, but upside down, as the tails of the cook's white pigeons strutting and preening on the cookhouse roof. Other birds were about now; a woodpecker with a scarlet head was busy on a casuarina; a pair of hoopoes pecked and dipped on the lawns. Inside the house, Christabel, our tame hill mynah bird, whistled and swore at her cousins outside; mynahs were countless as sparrows in England. The smell of dew-wet earth came up and of smoke, burning wood and dung.

Presently Hannah, her bone bangles softly chinking, came along the top verandah carrying trays of tea and toast for adults, bananas for children. Then she dressed Rose who was always first out in the early morning, but it was only a few minutes before we three elder ones had gobbled down our bananas and rushed out to meet the day.

Early mornings seem more precious in India than any-where else; it is not only the freshness before the heat, the colours muted by the light, the sparkle of dew; it is the time for cleansing and for prayer. From the first paling of the sky, figures with bare legs, a brass lota-pot in their hands, had been going down to the river or to the water tanks for ritual bathing and to say their prayers. Men and women went into the water in their dhotis or saris and washed these too as they wore them, then stood waist deep, water dripping from their joined hands as they faced the rising sun. They were Hindus but, even before dawn, the muezzins had given their call from the minaret of the mosque this side of the river, echoed a moment after from the mosque on the far bank and, as the sun came up, the Muslims, wherever they were, unrolled their prayer mats.

As she pushed Rose's perambulator along, Hannah was saying her rosary—she could answer Rose and murmur de-cades at the same time.

The gardeners, having finished the paths, were flailing the grass with long flexible bamboos to remove the dew; if it were left the grass would scorch when the sun was high. Out-side on the road, the water sprinkler went majestically by, drawn by its white bullock with the utmost slowness; on the bustee side of the tank buffaloes were being washed, blissfully cool and wet, before their long hot day of toil began; goats and kids were released—as we were. Not much in the way of morning ritual was required of us.

"Wash behind your ears," Aunt Mary would call from her bed as she drank tea, and we splashed in the basin, then buttoned one another up, folded our pyjamas, turned down our beds. We did little praying; there was no Aunt Evelyn Kate in Narayangunj. We were free of everyone and everything and, as hares take on the colour of their surroundings, we disappeared, each going our separate ways except during the period of Nana, when we were taken for a walk every morning.

Mam and Aunt Mary only went for a walk if they could first drive out into the surrounding country; to walk from the house meant going through the bazaar—"That smelly bazaar," they said. Of course it smelled; it was early morning and the people were urinating or cleaning, sweeping out their houses, emptying buckets of cess and rubbish in the road, spitting as they cleaned their teeth with a neemstick under the communal tap or blowing their noses with their fingers; or else they were cooking, curries with oil and garlic or frying chappattis, unleavened dough, or making pooriahs, vegetables fried in butter; all of which made our stomachs rumble—what were a few bananas and a piece of toast? But however hungry we were, we knew that to eat or drink anything in the bazaar, even a piece of fruit or a jilibi, meant instant punishment—and a dose of castor oil—besides the flies were a little thick. Flies swarmed over everything, hung round the bullocks' sores and crawled round the babies' eyes.

In the bazaar temple with its pointed silver roof, silver because it was covered with beaten-out kerosene tins, the Gods were being got up too. As images of Rama and Sita, the celestial lovers, this temple had two large jointed dolls with black wigs and eyes that opened and shut—much better dolls than ours. The priest dressed them; sometimes they wore tinselled crowns and sat in a swing while the people came to pray and offered them flowers, sugar and rice.

We went through the bazaar on our morning rides. When we, Jon and Rumer, came to Narayangunj, we knew how to ride, not with Nancy's natural style and dash, but how to sit a pony, how to rise to the trot and hold the reins, how to mount and dismount; Fa had taught us long ago in Assam, almost as soon as we could walk, side-saddle first as Mam was afraid that our short legs might bow; we could not remember learning. Apparently it never occurred to him to teach us any further. We rode for exercise, or simply to get from one place to another, as people rode when a horse was a necessity, and rode as we were, in our cotton dresses—no jodhpurs, velvet caps or hacking jackets for us—rode too as naturally as we walked; but neither Fa nor Aunt Mary, who was a good horsewoman and had her own riding mare, ever took us out with them, ever schooled us or took us over jumps. Two of us, Jon, Rumer or Nancy, went out every early morning. "If you have a pony you must ride it," Fa told us, so we took it in turns to ride. Another pony had appeared for Jon and Rumer to share, a small country-bred crossed with Arab and snowily white. We called her Pearl; Nancy's was smaller, a chestnut called Ruby.

"Why should Nancy have a pony all to herself?"

"It was hers when you were left in England."

"Why wasn't she left in England?"

"She was too small."

"Then why did she have to have a pony?"

What puzzles now is not the fact that we had ponies but the way in which we rode them. With a syce walking beside each pony we passed through the bazaar at a sedate walk, trotted up the Dacca road, had a brief canter across a field for as long as the syces could keep up, turned and came home. We petted Ruby and Pearl, fed them with sugar cane, sometimes played circuses or covered-wagons with them, but that was all, although Nancy went to the stables with Fa to watch the evening feeds. Few children can have learned as little or got as little fun from their ponies and in the early mornings we did not want to ride—we wanted to play.

All the time we were in India we were fanatics for play, and the early mornings were a halcyon time for it because no authoritative grown-up was about; they were sipping their morning tea, reading, or getting up with grown people's extraordinary slowness and elaboration. Fa had to shave, and pulled gruesome faces as he did it while Jetta stood by with the lathering stick; then he had to have a bath. Mam and Aunt Mary did up their hair in countless rolls and puffs, brushing separate locks round pads called "rats" which did look rather like limbless and tailless rat bodies. The servants were busy, but in the garden all was peace.

There should still be children's voices in that garden:

"I won't be Crusoe's goat, I want to be a person."

"You can't. There wasn't another person. There wasn't anybody on the island except Crusoe and Man Friday."

"Can't Man Friday have a wife?" Though wives were not popular. "Can't he?"

"He can't because he didn't. I know—you can be the parrot."

Rose had a kind of option but Nancy was always made to play. She tried to protest. "I don't want to be Puck. Can't I ever be Titania?"

Titania was an exception among wives: we all wanted to be Titania.

"I don't want to be a Roundhead . . . a Paleface . . . a German . . . ."

"I don't want to be the man in the barrel who went over Niagara Falls."

A feast would be laid out on the side steps: earth and water rissoles, chopped flower-petal rice, daisy-head poached eggs on grass spinach.

"Shall I go and ask Mustapha for some real milk?" But real milk would have spoilt it. "I'll go and milk the poinsettias." This was not as whimsical as it sounds. The poinsettia stems had sap like milk, white and sticky.

We did not often play with dolls; we made babies out of pillows with shoe-button eyes and red ribbon tongues; they were more cuddlesome than dolls but had to be given back in the evening which was tiresome. Rose for a while had a tiny pink potato with matchstick legs; she called it Nebuchadnezzar and kept it till it went mouldy.

"But why do you turn things into something else all the time?" people asked us. We did not know why, but a croquet set became a family of thin grown-ups, fat children; our guinea-pigs were flocks of sheep grazing over the tennis court, herded by David and Jonathan; in Darjeeling we had outsize stag beetles, called by us "crutchies", and these were racehorses. Grown people, though, seldom saw much of our play; the tacit understanding was to keep them out.

"What are you playing?"

"Nothing".

Or, if that were too palpable a lie we would give a camouflage answer like Mothers and Fathers, which we never played, or, with us, another improbable play, Shops. "Shops," we said with bland eyes. Nothing can be more baffling than the eyes of little girls. Yet if we had told what we were playing no one would have been much the wiser because our plays were like icebergs, only three-tenths seen, the rest hidden, inside ourselves. It was what we thought into our play that made its spell.

"Where are the children?"

The answer might have been, "In the tomato bed."

The tomato bed was odorous and hot; its high plants made thickets of green shade through which the light filtered down into a tropical forest. Nitai's bantams which strayed there were the pygmies; the tomatoes, mostly green because they would not ripen down below, were gourds; their yellow five-pointed star flowers were rare orchids on tall trees while the white hard-baked Bengali earth of the potato patch was the desert beyond.

Sometimes the tennis court was surrounded by sea and became an island. "Who lit a fire, a fire on the tennis court?" exploded Fa. We knew who it was: it was Jon, but in answer to Fa's question there was silence, and all three of us, Jon, Rumer and Nancy, were sent to bed which did not matter because if Jon were punished we preferred to be punished too.

One year the circus came to Narayangunj for a single night's performance before going on to Dacca; such excitements were rare and from the moment we saw the posters we talked of that circus, dreamed of it.

"Real lions!" said Nancy—she had never seen a lion.

"Liberty horses," said Jon, but she chose that very day to be her naughtiest—it sometimes seemed as if she had to spoil what she wanted most—and she went from bad to worse until the inevitable happened, "Very well! You won't go to the circus," said Mam. None of us would go, either, not even when Fa said we must.

Why did Jon have such power? For one thing, if her temper were roused she was afraid of nothing and no one. "Jon really throws things," Rumer would warn and, in her small way, Jon was a firebrand; the temper came up in a moment and, with the temper, words flowed, winged words that cut more sharply than she knew.

"She says such things!" Miss Andrews wept to Mam when she gave her notice. "She knows just how to hurt."

In Nana, Jon met her match; they would fight like two cocks; with Hannah she was gentle; but Jon's rule over us was not one of fear, though we had a healthy respect for her; if she bullied she also protected, and though she was so clearly a leader she was the least smug or self-satisfied of girls. Nancy and Rumer once heard grown people talking at a party about Jon, saying what a beautiful child she was and debated whether or not Jon should be told. "We don't want to make her conceited," said Rumer.

"Oh, tell. Tell her. Tell her," begged Nancy who could not bear anything pleasant to be kept back, but when Jon was told she simply did not believe it.

Above all, Jon was interesting, as unexpected as she was gifted; our plays would have been nothing without her, we knew it and seldom rebelled.

"I'm Oberon, Rumer's Titania. You must be Puck," ordered Jon. Nancy was Puck and, as we played, forgot she had ever wanted to be anyone else.

In the mornings it was only the empty-drum feeling of our stomachs that at last drove us in; by eight o'clock, when Azad Ali sounded the gong, the emptiness was acute.

There was never anything more pleasant than our family breakfasts, set in the garden or in the dining-room with all of us round the big table. Every day there was a clean cloth— . why not? We had our own dhobi—and in the middle of it a bowl of fresh flowers; Mam did the flowers with Govind before breakfast. The food was delicious, and Jon and Rumer remembered the stale London eggs, the horrible porridge; in Narayangunj we had kedgeree or rice and dhal with poached eggs; we were and have always remained true Bengali rice eaters. Sometimes we had fish cakes or rumble tumble, the Indian name for scrambled eggs; always and best of all there was fruit: papayas golden-fleshed and full of black seeds that were supposed to hold all the vitamins but which we never ate: oranges that felt still warm from the tree: kulu apples, bananas as many as we wanted. Mangoes and lichees ripened in the hot weather when we usually were away in the Hills but sometimes Fa would send us a basketful.

There was never any hurry at those breakfasts, no bus or train to catch to school or office, nothing to impinge. The post did not come until midday so there were no tiresome letters to engross grown-up attention, likewise no newspapers until the mail steamers brought them. Offices could not open early because the babus, the clerks, had to do the family shopping before they came to work; good-class women do not do the marketing in India and, in the climate, household shopping has to be freshly done each day.

It was not until after nine that Maxim came round and Fa's office boxes were carried out and put in the trap that waited, its high yellow wheels and polished brass glittering in the sun. Fa came out, sprang up on the high step, took the reins and long-lashed whip; Maxim snorted as the syce let his head go and was off almost before Fa had sat down, while the syce, the tail of his turban flying, ran after and took a flying leap up behind. It was a far more impressive setting off than any car could have given. We, having waved from the steps, were sent off to the bathroom.

There are said to be privies built for three; they had

nothing on us. True, we each had our own commode made of wood with an enamel pan that lifted out, but we all went to the bathroom together and called this time The Thunderbox Club. The pans were shallow, the boxes high so that they were for the most part hollow and, standing on short legs in the cavernous bathroom, splendidly reverberant. We knew all about drums, the excitement of tomtoms, and we drummed with our heels as we sat, while, with pieces of lavatory paper wrapped round combs, we played harmoniums.

Rose, being young, did not have a thunderbox but a small enamel pot on the floor; she was something of a clown and would bump it along the floor and up and down as she sat while we all egged her on. With gales of laughter we tried to see who could say the most outrageous things until the whole atmosphere became a little bawdy; perhaps the Godden Aunts had been right when they insisted that even Rumer at five must be alone, though the Randolph Gardens lavatory had a slippery mahogany seat like a shelf and an immense blue willow-pattern pan with a brass bottom that opened into darkness. "It goes right down the sewers to the Thames," Jon had told Rumer which frightened her so badly she could hardly ever perform naturally and had to be dosed with emulsion and syrup of figs almost every night.

There were no sewers in Narayangunj, no plumbing in the house beyond a few cold water taps that dripped a trickle of water. When the pots had been used, Nitai, or his sweeper wife, came with a covered basket to remove and empty them in a limed pit and wash them out with disinfectant. It is not a pleasant idea that one class in the community should do this work—the carrying of night soil as it is called—but it is a custom of the country and Nitai, our old sweeper, was a respected member of the household: indeed his wife was called the "mata rani"—the sweeper queen. The thunder-boxes were scrupulously clean, practical, comfortable and above all friendly, but the Club only lasted as long as Nana. To Nana there was nothing wrong in a relaxed mateyness; had she not once been with an Anglo-Indian family where there was one toothbrush between eleven children? "But that was too much," said Nana. "Not nice at all." Directly she was gone and Hannah took command, the Thunderbox Club was reported and we were banished to separate bathrooms—there were plenty in the house—and made to have more restrained and girl-becoming ways.

After breakfast and bathroom, Jon and Rumer took it in turn to help Mam to interview the cook and give out the stores. . .

. . .While one of us, Jon or Rumer, was attending on this morning ceremonial the other, after getting the lesson table ready, was undergoing a music lesson from Aunt Mary— undergoing was the right word. Neither of us was musical, but up and down on the old upright piano went the scales, the thumb going under with a thump and a jerk. Small fingers can sound like iron hammers and our poundings must have gone through Aunt Mary's head—she far too often had a headache—and she used a ruler, only a light one, not one of those heavy round ones, on our knuckles, sometimes on our heads. It did not hurt but we resented it and took our revenge in public by pretending to cower whenever she raised her hand. She rapped and we hammered and kicked the panels of the piano—we could not reach the pedals—and she rapped again; it was always estranged, and strained, that we came down into the garden for our other lessons.

There were two camps in the garden: one with comfortable garden chairs, a low table and stool and a rug spread with toys was for Mam and the little ones; the other, removed under a distant tree, had a high bamboo table, three upright dining-room chairs round it and was made ready in a business-like fashion with books, ink, blotting paper and sewing bags; it was for Aunt Mary and us big ones.

A garden is no place for lessons; there is too much going on. This was especially so in ours: an oriole flashed past; a long-tailed tree-pie gave his liquid call of "Chocolate! Chocolate!" Above us in the dark recesses of the mango tree lived a family of dear little owls. Two gardeners had a quarrel; the dhobi and his wife and five or six of their sons spread washing on the grass to bleach; a hawker argued with Guru and, once a year, always in the morning when we had begun lessons, the gate would open to let in the mattress man and his assistant, carrying big bundles of fresh cotton and the strange-looking wood and bamboo instruments of their trade. Tall and solemn, wearing white, they would stalk to their own spot under the line of neem trees, seat themselves on the ground, and wait for all our mattresses and pillows to be brought to them by Mustapha and Abedul. Out of the corner of our eyes, while we pretended to listen to Aunt Mary, we would watch each mattress being emptied of its stuffing, see the cotton being beaten and aired, tossed high in the sunshine, before it was put back again, augmented when necessary. Tufts of cotton came across the garden to us on the breeze, alighting tantalizingly on our table and we would see Nancy, free as air, streak across the lawn to join the busy party in the dappled neem shade. She would squat there, watching the cotton fly, or help to spread the white piles on bamboo mats in the sunshine.

"Why doesn't Nancy do lessons?"

"She does."

"Only for an hour, and with Mam."

"She's only five—or six—seven—eight or nine," as the years passed.

The truth was that Nancy was impossible to teach, not because she was stupid, or backward, but because it was only on the wing, as it were, that she would learn anything. She was to defeat governess after governess, school after school, and how she learned to read, write and add up was a miracle. She even defeated Mam.

"Nancy, what does R-A-T spell?"

"Rat."

"C-A-T?"

"Cat."

"M-A-T?"

The brown eyes would have wandered to a hawk up in the far skies, or a butterfly on the morning glory.

"M-A-T, Nancy. You know rat and cat, now M-A-T."

"Sailor," said Nancy.

From *Two Under the Indian Sun* (1966)

A Family on the Move

GERALD DURRELL

Practically all Gerald Durrell's books are hilarious and this one about his own family is no exception. Here they have decided that living in England is cold, expensive and ridiculous, so off they go to Greece . . .

July had been blown out like a candle by a biting wind that ushered in a leaden August sky. A sharp stinging drizzle fell, billowing into opaque grey sheets when the wind caught it. Along the Bournemouth sea-front the beach-huts turned blank wooden faces towards a greeny-grey, froth-chained sea that leapt eagerly at the cement bulwark of the shore. The gulls had been tumbled inland over the town, and they now drifted above the house-tops on taut wings, whining peevishly. It was the sort of weather calculated to try anyone's endurance.

Considered as a group, my family was not a very prepossessing sight that afternoon, for the weather had brought with it the usual selection of ills to which we were prone. For me, lying on the floor, labelling my collection of shells, it had brought catarrh, pouring into my skull like cement, so that I was forced to breathe stertorously through open mouth. For my brother Leslie, hunched dark and glowering by the fire, it had inflamed the convolutions of his ears so that they bled delicately but persistently. To my sister Margo it had delivered a fresh dappling of acne spots to a face that was already blotched like a red veil. For my mother there was a rich, bubbling cold, and a twinge of rheumatism to season it. Only my eldest brother, Larry, was untouched, but it was sufficient that he was irritated by our failings.

It was Larry, of course, who started it. The rest of us felt too apathetic to think of anything but our own ills, but Larry was designed by Providence to go through life like a small, blond firework, exploding ideas in other people's minds, and then curling up with a cat-like unctuousness and refusing to take any blame for the consequences. He had become increasingly irritable as the afternoon wore on. At length, glancing moodily round the room, he decided to attack Mother, as being the obvious cause of the trouble.

"Why do we stand this bloody climate?" he asked suddenly, making a gesture towards the rain-distorted window. "Look at it! And if it comes to that, look at us. . . . Margo swollen up like a plate of scarlet porridge. . .Leslie wandering round with fourteen fathoms of cotton-wool in each ear. . . Gerry sounds as though he's had a cleft palate from birth. . . And look at you: you're looking more decrepit and hag-ridden every day."

Mother peered over the top of a large volume entitled *Easy Recipes from Rajputana*.

"Indeed I'm not," she said indignantly.

"You *are*," Larry insisted; "you're beginning to look like an Irish washerwoman. . .and your family looks like a series of illustrations from a medical encyclopedia."

Mother could think of no really crushing reply to this, so she contented herself with a glare before retreating once more behind her book.

"What we need is sunshine," Larry continued; "don't you agree, Les?. . .Les. . . *Les!*"

Leslie unravelled a large quantity of cotton-wool from one ear.

"What d'you say?" he asked.

"There you are!" said Larry, turning triumphantly to Mother, "it's becoming a major operation to hold a conversation with him. I ask you, what a position to be in! One brother can't hear what you say, and the other one can't be understood. Really, it's time something was done. I can't be expected to produce deathless prose in an atmosphere of gloom and eucalyptus."

"Yes, dear," said Mother vaguely.

"What we all need," said Larry, getting into his stride again, "is sunshine. . .a country where we can *grow*."

"Yes, dear, that would be nice," agreed Mother, not really listening.

"I had a letter from George this morning—he say's Corfu's wonderful. Why don't we pack up and go to Greece?"

"Very well, dear, if you like," said Mother unguardedly.

Where Larry was concerned she was generally very careful not to commit herself.

"When?" asked Larry, rather surprised at this cooperation.

Mother, perceiving that she had made a tactical error, cautiously lowered *Easy Recipes from Rajputana*.

"Well, I think it would be a sensible idea if you were to go on ahead, dear, and arrange things. Then you can write and tell me if it's nice, and we all can follow," she said cleverly.

Larry gave her a withering look.

"You said *that* when I suggested going to Spain," he reminded her, "and I sat for two interminable months in Seville, waiting for you to come out, while you did nothing except write me massive letters about drains and drinking water, as though I was the Town Clerk or something. No, if we're going to Greece, let's all go together."

"You do *exaggerate*, Larry," said Mother plaintively; "anyway, I can't go just like that. I have to arrange something about this house."

"Arrange? Arrange what, for heaven's sake? Sell it."

"I can't do that, dear," said Mother, shocked.

"Why not?"

"But I've only just bought it."

"Sell it while it's still untarnished, then."

"Don't be ridiculous, dear," said Mother firmly; "that's quite out of the question. It would be madness."

So we sold the house and fled from the gloom of the English summer, like a flock of migrating swallows.

We all travelled light, taking with us only what we considered to be the bare essentials of life. When we opened our luggage for Customs inspection, the contents of our bags were a fair indication of character and interests. Thus Margo's luggage contained a multitude of diaphanous garments, three books on slimming, and a regiment of small bottles each containing some elixir guaranteed to cure acne. Leslie's case held a couple of roll-top pullovers and a pair of trousers which were wrapped round two revolvers, an air-pistol, a book called *Be Your Own Gunsmith*, and a large bottle of oil that leaked. Larry was accompanied by two trunks of books and a brief-case containing his clothes. Mother's luggage was sensibly divided between clothes and various volumes on cooking and gardening. I travelled with only those items that I thought necessary to relieve the tedium of a long journey: four books on natural history, a butterfly net, a dog, and a jam-jar full of caterpillars all in imminent danger of turning into chrysalids. Thus, by our standards fully equipped, we left the clammy shores of England. . . .

(*They have arrived on Corfu:*)

We threaded our way out of the noise and confusion of the Customs shed into the brilliant sunshine on the quay. Around us the town rose steeply, tiers of multi-coloured houses piled haphazardly, green shutters folded back from their windows, like the wings of a thousand moths. Behind us lay the bay, smooth as a plate, smouldering with that unbelievable blue.

Larry walked swiftly, with head thrown back and an expression of such regal disdain on his face that one did not notice his diminutive size, keeping a wary eye on the porters who struggled with his trunks. Behind him strolled Leslie, short, stocky, with an air of quiet belligerence, and then Margo, trailing yards of muslin and scent. Mother, looking like a tiny, harassed missionary in an uprising, was dragged unwillingly to the nearest lamp-post by an exuberant Roger, and was forced to stand there, staring into space, while he relieved pent-up feelings that had accumulated in his kennel. Larry chose two magnificently dilapidated horse-drawn cabs, had the luggage installed in one, and seated himself in the second. Then he looked round irritably.

"Well?" he asked. "What are we waiting for?"

"We're waiting for Mother," explained Leslie. "Roger's found a lamp-post."

"Dear God!" said Larry, and then hoisted himself upright in the cab and bellowed, "Come *on*, Mother, come on. Can't the dog wait?"

"Coming, dear," called Mother passively and untruthfully, for Roger showed no sign of quitting the post.

"That dog's been a damned nuisance all the way," said Larry.

"Don't be so impatient," said Margo indignantly; "the dog can't help it. . .and anyway, we had to wait an hour in Naples for *you*."

"My stomach was out of order," explained Larry coldly.

"Well, presumably *his* stomach's out of order," said Margo triumphantly. "It's six of one and a dozen of the other."

"You mean half-a-dozen of the other."

"Whatever I mean, it's the same thing."

At this moment Mother arrived, slightly dishevelled, and we had to turn our attention to the task of getting Roger into the cab. He had never been in such a vehicle, and treated it with suspicion. Eventually we had to lift him bodily and hurl him inside, yelping frantically, and then pile in breathlessly after him and hold him down. The horse, frightened by this activity, broke into a shambling trot, and we ended in a tangled heap on the floor of the cab with Roger moaning loudly underneath us.

"What an entry," said Larry bitterly. "I had hoped to give an impression of gracious majesty, and this is what happens . . .we arrive in town like a troupe of medieval tumblers."

"Don't keep *on*, dear," Mother said soothingly, straightening her hat; "we'll soon be at the hotel."

So our cab clopped and jingled its way into the town, while we sat on the horsehair seats and tried to muster the appearance of gracious majesty Larry required. Roger, wrapped in Leslie's powerful arms, lolled his head over the side of the vehicle and rolled his eyes as though at his last gasp. Then we rattled past an alleyway in which four scruffy mongrels were lying in the sun. Roger stiffened, glared at them and let forth a torrent of deep barks. The mongrels were immediately galvanised into activity, and they sped after the cab, yapping vociferously. Our pose was irretrievably shattered, for it took two people to restrain the raving Roger, while the rest of us leaned out of the cab and made wild gestures with magazines and books at the pursuing horde. This only had the effect of exciting them still further, and at each alley-way we passed their numbers increased, until by the time we were rolling down the main thoroughfare of the town there were some twenty-four dogs swirling about our wheels, almost hysterical with anger.

"Why doesn't somebody do something?" asked Larry, raising his voice above the uproar. "This is like a scene from *Uncle Tom's Cabin*."

"Why don't you do something, instead of criticizing?" snapped Leslie, who was locked in combat with Roger.

Larry promptly rose to his feet, snatched the whip from our astonished driver's hand, made a wild swipe at the herd of dogs, missed them, and caught Leslie across the back of the neck.

"What the hell d'you think you're playing at?" Leslie snarled, twisting a scarlet and angry face towards Larry.

"Accident," explained Larry airily. "I'm out of practice. . . it's so long since I used a horse-whip."

"Well, watch what you're bloody well doing," said Leslie loudly and belligerently.

"Now, now, dear, it was an accident," said Mother.

Larry took another swipe at the dogs and knocked off Mother's hat.

"You're more trouble than the dogs," said Margo.

"Do be careful, dear," said Mother, clutching her hat; "you might hurt someone. I should put the whip down."

At that moment the cab shambled to a halt outside a doorway over which hung a board with Pension Suisse inscribed on it. The dogs, feeling that they were at last going to get to grips with this effeminate black canine who rode in cabs, surrounded us in a solid, panting wedge. The door of the hotel opened and an ancient bewhiskered porter appeared and stood staring glassily at the turmoil in the street. The difficulties of getting Roger out of the cab and into the hotel were considerable, for he was a heavy dog, and it took the combined efforts of the family to lift, carry, and restrain him. Larry had by now forgotten his majestic pose and was rather enjoying himself. He leapt down and danced about the pavement with the whip, cleaving a path through the dogs, along which Leslie, Margo, Mother and I hurried, bearing the struggling, snarling Roger. We staggered into the hall, and the porter slammed the front door and leant against it, his moustache quivering. The manager came forward, eyeing us with a mixture of apprehension and curiosity. Mother faced him, hat on one side of her head, clutching in one hand my jam-jar of caterpillars.

"Ah!" she said, smiling sweetly, as though our arrival had been the most normal thing in the world. "Our name's Durrell. I believe you've got some rooms booked for us?"

"Yes, madame," said the manager, edging round the still grumbling Roger; "they are on the first floor. . .four rooms and a balcony."

"How nice," beamed Mother; "then I think we'll go straight up and have a little rest before lunch."

And with considerable majestic graciousness she led her family upstairs. . . .

From *My Family and Other Animals* (1956)

Only Child

ANON

Upon a hill a roofless house—
Beyond that house the sea;
And in that house and on that shore
A ghostly family.

I see them scamper up the stairs
To play with haunted toys—
Seven, I count: four frilly girls,
Three knickerbockered boys.
The oldest boy is Algernon,
The others Tom and Claude;
The girls are Jane and little Nan,
Caroline and kind Maud.

I race behind them on the sands,
Outstretched to grab a sleeve,
But always they have reached the cliff
And I must stamp and grieve.

Jeering, they scale the rocky path,
But one of them is kind—
It's Maud who always turns to wave
At me left far behind.

I'll be long gone but they'll be there,
The house, perhaps, no more,
And still some child with listening ears
Shall hear them on the shore;
And still they'll mock that vain pursuit,
And still Maud will be kind—
Turning to smile and faintly wave
To one left far behind.

Upon the hill a ruined house,
Beyond its stones the sea;
And ghostly in and out of time
A happy family. . .

Acknowledgements

The Editor and Hamish Hamilton Ltd. are grateful to the following copyright holders for permission to use copyright material: The author, Ursula Moray Williams, and Curtis Brown Ltd., London, for permission to include *Prayer for a Happy Family*; Frederick Warne & Co. Ltd., London, for permission to include *The Poor Cottages* from LITTLE LORD FAUNTLEROY by Frances Hodgson Burnett; The Literary Trustees of Walter de la Mare and the Society of Authors, London, as their representative for permission to include *The Little Creature* and *Five of Us* from THE COMPLETE POEMS OF WALTER DE LA MARE; The Clarendon Press, Oxford, for permission to include *Margaret Paston to her Son, John* from THE PASTON LETTERS, edited by Norman Davis, © 1958 Oxford University Press; Faber & Faber Ltd., London, for permission to include *The Easter Egg* from THE COUNTRY CHILD by Alison Uttley; Hogarth Press Ltd., London, and William Morrow & Co., Inc., New York, for permission to include *The Kitchen* from CIDER WITH ROSIE (U.S. title THE EDGE OF THE DAY) by Laurie Lee; Brockhampton Press Ltd. for permission to include *A Fly-Away Family* from PETER PAN by J. M. Barrie; His Honour Sir Adrian Curlewis and Ward Lock & Co. Ltd., London, for permission to include *The General Sees Active Service* from SEVEN LITTLE AUSTRALIANS by Ethel Turner; Lady Herbert and A. P. Watt & Son, London, for permission to include *The Lucky Baby* from PLAIN JANE by A. P. Herbert; John Farquharson Ltd.,

255

London, and the Estate of E. Nesbit for permission to include *Being Wanted* from FIVE CHILDREN AND IT by E. Nesbit; Frederick Muller Ltd., London, and Vanguard Press Inc., New York, for permission to include *The Baby Show* from THE FAMILY AT ONE END STREET by Eve Garnett; Harvey Unna Ltd., London, and the author for permission to include *The Smell of Privet* from THE SMELL OF PRIVET by Barbara Sleigh; Macmillan, London, and Viking Press, Inc., New York, for permission to include *The Web of the Day* from TWO UNDER THE INDIAN SUN by Jon and Rumer Godden, © 1966 by Jon Godden and Rumer Godden; Granada Publishing Ltd., London, and Viking Press, Inc., New York, for permission to include *A Family on the Move* from MY FAMILY AND OTHER ANIMALS by Gerald Durrell © 1956 by Gerald M. Durrell.

The Editor and Hamish Hamilton Ltd. have made every effort to trace the holders of copyright in all extracts included in this anthology. If any query should arise, it should be addressed to the Publishers.